WHEN TORCS FLY

The Petralist

WHEN TORCS FLY

The Petralist

FRANK MORIN

Whipsaw Press

When Torcs Fly
A Petralist Novella

ISBN: 978-1-946910-01-1

A Whipsaw Press Original

Edited by Joshua Essoe
(http://www.joshuaessoe.com/)

Cover art by Kathryn Renta
(http://www.latchkeyarist.com/)

Book design by Kathryn Morin

First Whipsaw printing: May 2018

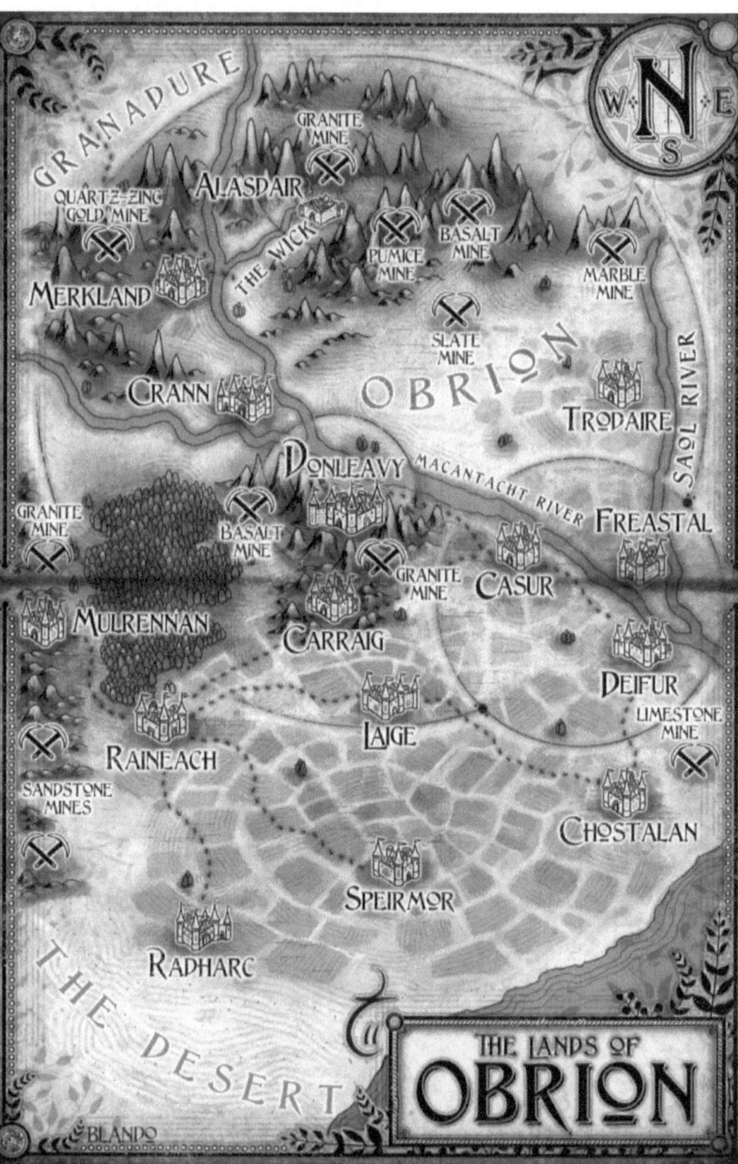

N
W E
S
GRANADURE
GRANITE MINE
ALASDAIR
QUARTZ-ZINC GOLD MINE
THE WICK
PUMICE MINE
BASALT MINE
MARBLE MINE
MERKLAND
SLATE MINE
OBRION
CRANN
TRODAIRE
DONLEAVY
MACANTACHT RIVER
SAOL RIVER
FREASTAL
GRANITE MINE
BASALT MINE
GRANITE MINE
CASUR
MULRENNAN
CARRAIG
DEIFUR
LIMESTONE MINE
RAINEACH
LAIGE
SANDSTONE MINES
CHOSTALAN
SPEIRMOR
RADHARC
THE DESERT
BLANDO
THE LANDS OF
OBRION

Wick Tor
loch Sholto
Mount Alasdair
Mount Ingram
loch kadhar
Upper Wick
Alasdair
Powder house
River Barges
Lord Gavin's Manor house
loch Wick
Lower Wick
the valley
BLANDÖ
N
The LANDS OF ALASDAIR

CHAPTER ONE

The Risk of Writing Things Down

omas entered the training yard with a confident stride, ready for his day of glory. His leather battle armor creaked, and his granite curse skittered across his body, like kittens kneading at the underside of his skin. It itched as if he hadn't washed in weeks, but that was easy to ignore.

He crossed the packed sand ground toward the two dozen other Boulders assembled to compete for their chance to win places in the newly-formed elite fighting company. They all won their first round competitions to prove they were the best fighters in High Lord Dougal's army.

Well, most of them were.

Cameron was a brutish-faced, burly soldier, and he actually looked like he believed he belonged there. He grunted when Tomas joined the group. "How'd you survive the first round, flatlander? They give you a crippled old lady to fight?"

That triggered a round of laughter, and Tomas hoped he'd get to duel Cameron as his round two test. The man was a talented bash fighter, but he couldn't seem to accept the possibility that an outsider might just win one of the coveted seats. He just wasn't smart enough to be a Fast Roller.

So Tomas grinned. "Fast Rollers have to do more than break rocks with their faces."

Cameron's smile turned predatory and the expandable leather plates of his armor creaked and scraped as he tapped a little granite and his muscles swelled with impending violence. "Round two is going to be fun."

"I love your optimism."

Cameron whistled between the gap in his front teeth. "You're taking quite a risk using a word that big so early in the morning."

"I'll take my chances." Tomas doubted he'd need much heavy thinking during the next round anyway.

Sergeant Rory exited the nearby command post and approached the assembled hopefuls. The craggy-faced sergeant was easily the best fighter after Captain Hector in all of High Lord Dougal's army. He was a rising star, and Tomas could not imagine a better leader to train the new company.

It was a beautiful morning for the second round of the culling process. Warm sunlight made the worn sand of the training yard gleam like gold. Gray stone walls surrounded the fifty-yard-square yard, dwarfed by the gleaming spires of Merkland's majestic central palace that filled the sky beyond.

Rory spoke, his voice like stones tumbling in a wooden box. "Congratulations men. You all passed the first round but that was the easy part." The hint of a smile broke the hard contours of his face. "Now the real fun begins. The Fast Rollers are not just bash fighters. We are the elite of High Lord Dougal's forces. We are the hammer against the Grandurian threat, and we will destroy the so-called 'Crushers' Wolfram is developing."

Tomas joined in an enthusiastic cheer, eager to see who else would win their places with him in the ranks of Rory's company. He loved bash fighting better than almost anything else in the world, and the Fast Rollers would get the best bash fighting of all.

His own high lord had sent him north to the rugged, beautiful lands of Merkland almost a year ago as part of an exchange with High Lord Dougal. If Tomas could secure a spot in the Fast Rollers, he would guarantee permanent residence. He couldn't imagine returning to boring Raineach. Here soldiers had to be strong to face the looming Grandurian threat so close to the north. Here, Tomas might get a chance to test himself against those legendary Petralists. No matter what it took, how many duels he had to win, he would become a Fast Roller.

Rory raised his hand for quiet. "You've all proven yourselves as Boulders, but Fast Rollers need to be more. Some of our missions will include infiltrating enemy camps, either to collect intelligence or to remove high profile targets. The next round of testing will give all of you a chance to prove that you can think on your feet, that your brains are not just a bunch of rocks crushed into that gray space, and that you're ready for higher forms of combat. Sergeant Munro will see to issuing orders for your partnerships."

Partners? No one had said anything about needing a partner.

Rory must have noted their expressions because he added, "Fast Rollers work as a team. Our basic units are partnerships. Captain Hector has pioneered advanced battle tactics, and he has proven that two well-trained Boulders working together are more than five times more effective than when working alone. So you will be assigned a partner, and that man will remain your partner from this time forward. Together you will either pass or fail the next test."

Tomas tried to suppress an unfamiliar feeling of nervousness. He was tempted to tap granite. The powdered stone, absorbed through his skin, fueled his curse and granted him and the other Boulders their remarkable strength and stone-hardened skin.

The crawling itch of his curse always helped him relax, but could he risk using it? He was not sure if they would be granted additional portions before the next round. He glanced around and confirmed that there was an even number of hopeful recruits. It would've been the Tallan's own luck to get cut from the competition only because Rory could not find him a partner.

Sergeant Munro, a competent, middle-aged Boulder who was one of the few fighters who was also a decent administrator, began calling out names and gesturing for the men to line up. Tomas eagerly stepped into the line when Munro called him.

When half the men were assembled, Munro ordered the remainder into a second line facing the first. Tomas wondered if they would have to fight again to win their partner, or if they'd just be assigned to partner with the men standing directly across from them. He would be fine with either option, but Munro decided to complicate things. He moved down the first line, pulling small papers out of a helmet and handing one to each man. The process looked completely random, but Tomas frowned at the little papers. To trust their fates to whatever was written on them seemed wrong. He couldn't read even his own name.

When Munro finished handing out papers, he bellowed, "All right then lads, Healer Marcas can help any of you who can't read figure out who your partner is supposed to be. Get cracking."

Most of the other men in his line joined Tomas, crowding around Marcus, holding those devilish little papers more nervously than sharp blades. Marcas was a grumpy, aging fellow in a white Healer's jacket, who muttered about their ignorance with every name he read. He didn't even take Tomas's paper, but just glanced at it.

"Cameron."

Tomas blinked, then glared at the paper. He couldn't have heard that right. "No, I'm Tomas. Just read the name."

Marcus rolled his eyes. "One too many concussions I suppose. Your partner is Cameron. Good luck."

"How can you be sure? You barely looked at it."

Marcus grunted. "Name's not that hard, boy. Cameron's your partner. Go bang your heads against a wall somewhere together."

As Marcus moved down the line, Tomas was tempted to swallow the cursed paper to hide the evidence. By the Tallan's knobby earlobes, how could he be partnered with that idiot?

Even though he hesitated to join Cameron, the truth became apparent to everyone a moment later. The other seven pairs of hopeful Fast Rollers quickly found their partners, and most of them huddled together, laughing, discussing bashing strategies, and congratulating each other on the assignment.

Cameron spit out a small stick that he had been chewing on as Tomas approached, and he scowled. "Captain's got it in for me. You'd think he'd have the decency to just tell me I didn't make the cut. This way is insulting."

"Insulting to me," Tomas retorted. "This isn't going to be just a bash fight, Cameron. We actually need to think on this one."

Cameron grimaced. "Tallan only knows, but I'm not sure I can do the thinking for both of us."

"As if you've ever had an original thought in your life."

"Course I have," Cameron said with a little chuckle. "I was the one who figured out dating a blind woman was my best chance."

Tomas had to admit, that was a pretty good idea. "How many blind women are there in Merkland?"

"There is at least one."

"And she's actually letting you court her?"

Tomas hadn't expected to feel impressed. Despite the initial interest he'd sensed from more than a few women when he'd first arrived from the south, he had not yet managed to find a girl, or more importantly a girl's father willing to let him begin courting. Winning a spot in the Fast Rollers might change that.

Cameron shrugged. "Not sure, really. I might need to explain it better to her. The last time she hit me with a frying pan, I wasn't tapping granite and it actually dented my skull."

He rubbed the back of his head for emphasis.

"It's a good sign that she's such an energetic woman though," Tomas offered.

Cameron grinned and nodded.

Well, if Cameron could win any kind of woman, even if she was blind, maybe they had a chance after all. And if they could work together, that might silence his other critics even more thoroughly. Tomas blew out a breath and said, "Fine. Follow my lead and do exactly what I say, and maybe we can win through."

"You're cracked. I'm the senior new recruit," Cameron retorted.

"You have exactly the same rank I do," Tomas objected.

"Then why do you think they made you go get the paper?"

Tomas shrugged. "The leaders are always getting new orders."

Cameron shook his head and tapped the side of his nose. "Officers are always sending assistants to bring them the orders, like Rory does with Munro. You're my assistant, and if you serve me well I'll make sure I don't assign too much drudgery."

"That's not how a partnership works. We're supposed to work together and intimidate somebody else into doing the drudgery for us."

While Cameron considered that idea, Sergeant Rory raised his voice and drew their attention. "The battle master will provide additional portions. Munro will schedule your next test. Good luck, men. For those of you who make the cut, this day will mark the beginning of a whole new stage in your Guardian training."

CHAPTER TWO

Thinking Is Over-Rated

ameron stepped into the officer training courtyard, nestled in the crook of one sweeping arm of the central palace of Merkland. The large, stone-walled area was almost as big as the general training yard on the outskirts of town that they usually used. About eighty paces long and maybe fifty wide, it was covered with fine sand.

Since there weren't really that many officers, maybe they needed all that room so their brains didn't feel squeezed while they were doing all that thinking they were supposed to do all the time. Cameron rarely bothered to think, so he wasn't sure. He preferred to focus all of his strength on muscles used in actual fighting.

Tomas grunted as he joined Cameron. "I wonder why Rory is complicating things? I bet we can walk right through that door."

Cameron nodded as he studied the little structure on the far side of the yard, built for the purpose of the second-round challenge. The door did look flimsy. In fact, the walls wouldn't slow him down much either.

The rest of the open training yard was empty, but a row of officers stood atop the outer wall behind the little structure to observe their performance. Cameron decided to ignore them. They were supposed to pretend the structure was an enemy outpost, and even though the afternoon sun warmed his leather-clad shoulders, they'd been informed that it was night time, so they could approach without worry of being seen from a distance.

"The sergeant can think the deep thoughts," he said as he started toward the structure. "Orders are pretty simple. Sneak in there, subdue the defenders, pick up the artifact, and leave. I might not even need you on this one."

In fact, he'd prefer winning alone. It was insulting to have the flatlander as his companion. Tomas seemed to be a decent bash fighter, but Cameron had never tested his limits. He doubted anyone from the soft southern lands could max-tap granite as well as a local who had grown up in the rugged mountains of Dougal's realm.

Tomas rushed ahead of Cameron. "As if you could do it by yourself. I bet you still struggle to put your boots on the right feet in the morning."

"If they didn't want people confused, they shouldn't make both feet so similar." Cameron accelerated to pass Tomas, but his rude partner increased his own pace to stay ahead. "I might let you come along after all. You stink so bad, you might just knock them out before we even get inside."

Tomas actually stuck an arm out to prevent him passing and asked, "How many times did your mom have to slap you when you were born before she realized the ugly wouldn't come off?"

"I'm not really sure," Cameron admitted. "She told me that her hand started to hurt so my dad had to take over."

Tomas accelerated into a jog as Cameron tried to pull ahead again. "We're supposed to be infiltrating."

"Then slow down and let me take the lead like I'm supposed to."

Tomas chuckled as the two of them accelerated into a run, quickly drawing close to the structure they were supposed to sneak into. "You'll make a fine Fast Roller when you have to ask permission to pass someone."

"Captain Hector will throw you out for sure when he realizes you put your battle leathers on backward," Cameron retorted.

When Tomas faltered and glanced down to check, Cameron took the lead. He wasn't surprised that

Tomas fell for that one. All those plates and buckles and straps made the battle leathers ridiculously hard to put on in the morning. The fact that Cameron hadn't gotten it wrong in over a month had to be a sign that he deserved a place in the Fast Rollers.

Tomas broke into a sprint to catch up and actually pushed Cameron aside to retake the lead. So Cameron lashed out with a foot and caught Tomas's trailing heel, tripping him to the ground.

Tomas rolled back to his feet and shouted, "You kick like a girl and you fight like a coward."

Cameron slowed and turned to shout a curse back, but Tomas had already tapped his granite power. His muscles swelled with strength and the movable leather plates of his battle armor creaked as they expanded to handle his increased size. His skin faded to gray, becoming as hard as living stone. Tomas lunged, swinging a stone-hardened fist at Cameron's face.

He grinned and tapped granite too, twisting enough to let the blow slide past. Then as his body swelled with power, he threw a heavy punch into Tomas's midsection. That hit would have sent most Boulders tumbling, but Tomas barely staggered. He swept a jab into Cameron's chin.

Tomas might not be much of a partner, but turned out to be perhaps the best bash fighter Cameron had ever faced. He grinned as the two of them pounded on each other with unrestrained fury just outside the door to their objective. Cameron drew deep from granite until his muscles quivered with the need to strike and swelled to the point where they strained the limits of his battle leathers.

He let all of his concerns and worries go as he beat on Tomas, who matched him blow for blow. Thinking about thinking had started giving Cameron a headache, but all of that disappeared as he reveled in his element. For a moment, he forgot all about the mission and everything else and threw himself into a glorious, unrestrained bash fight.

Then Tomas caught him under the chin with a particularly good punch, staggering him back several paces. Tomas was right, that little wooden door barely slowed Cameron as he crashed through it.

He stumbled into the little room, shaking off splinters of wood, and his muscles shrank just enough for his mind to start working again and remember their mission. Inside the structure was even rougher than outside, containing one small cabinet, a rough wooden table, and three chairs. The three Boulders who had been waiting inside were already standing and facing the door.

"I don't think you two idiots understand what infiltration means," the one in the center laughed.

As his companions joined in the laughter, Tomas charged through the doorway, just missing Cameron. "Those big words won't protect you from my fist," he cried as he tackled the center defender right off his feet. The two of them smashed through the little table, and the distraction provided a wonderful opportunity for Cameron to punch the right-most defender through the nearest wall.

The three defenders were Boulders, but after fighting Tomas, they seemed more like basalt sniffers than bash fighters. It took only a moment for Cameron and Tomas to leave the three of them under a pile of splintered timbers, just about all that was left of the little structure they had been guarding.

Cameron grunted, "Someone should fire the carpenter who put this shack together. We barely gave it an excuse to fall down."

"That wasn't nearly as hard as I worried it was going to be," Tomas said as he stared down at the moaning defenders.

Cameron spotted an ornate wooden box under the rubble and scooped it up. It was scratched but only had five or six cracks in the top, so he figured that was a pretty good sign. "Maybe the next challenge will be a little more difficult."

Together they turned to leave, but stopped in surprise. Sergeant Rory and a full company of Fast Rollers stood assembled not ten paces away. Cameron decided that the astonished expressions on most of their faces meant that he and Tomas had done a particularly good job.

"You forgot to keep quiet," Rory growled and gestured at his assembled troops. "You roused the guard."

"I really hate complicated missions," Cameron said.

"Throw me," Tomas whispered as Rory and his company advanced. "I can get out with the box and we can still win."

"You're cracked. You'd win, not me."

"We're supposed to be a team. All that matters is getting the box out of here."

"Well I've got it, so why don't you throw me and sacrifice yourself?"

"We don't have time for this."

"Then let's just beat them all."

"Smartest thing you've said all day," Tomas said with a nod.

Cameron tucked the little box into a strap at the back of his battle armor. Bash fighting was one thing they could do together, and it was definitely easier than trying to think. He grinned and max-tapped granite.

"You've got to be kidding me," Rory said, his expression disbelieving.

Tomas swelled beside him. "Follow my lead."

"If you can get ahead of me." Cameron charged. He was the leader, and good leaders punched first.

They plunged into the Fast Rollers, but they were smart enough to angle away from Rory, who stood glaring in the center of the massed rank of soldiers. They attacked with all their fury, but it was like attacking a cliff. Instead of falling under Tomas and Cameron's furious assault like the three Boulders in the shack had, the Fast Rollers swarmed over the partners like a living avalanche.

In an embarrassingly short amount of time, the two of them lay bound in chains in the courtyard. The crowd of Fast Rollers parted and Rory stepped through, his craggy face disapproving.

"You two are talented bash fighters."

Cameron exchanged a happy look with Tomas. "Thank you, sir. Happy to be of service."

Rory barked a laugh. "I wouldn't call that performance a service. More an example of what not to do."

Tomas said, "You can count on us to always be ready for whatever you need. Even if it's not doing what needs to be done."

Rory stared at him, and for a second Cameron suspected the sergeant was amazed by their dedication.

Then Rory said, "Fast Rollers need to be more than bash fighters, and today you perfectly demonstrated you're not ready."

"But we got the box," Tomas protested.

"The mission was to infiltrate the room, steal the box, and escape with it." Rory spoke slowly, his expression darkening. "You two idiots roused every defender within a mile. If this had been a real mission, you would have died and probably gotten most of your squad killed along with you. Dismissed."

As Fast Rollers bent to release their bonds, Cameron couldn't believe what he was hearing. He couldn't have failed. He wanted to be a Fast Roller so bad, he could taste it. The dream was his favorite, and it tasted like sweetbreads dipped in cream. If he didn't become a Fast Roller, he'd never impress any woman long enough to court her.

"Sir, please," he begged, shaking off the last of the chains and struggling to his feet. "There has to be a way."

As Rory opened his mouth to respond, the nearby soldiers parted and snapped to attention. Captain Hector strode through, his expression unreadable. Tomas scrambled to his feet, and the two of them saluted in unison.

"Fast Rollers work in partnerships," Hector said, his voice calm, his gaze penetrating. Standing so close to the decorated soldier was inspiring. Well, it would be if he had been congratulating them on winning the challenge.

Swallowing his distaste for Tomas, Cameron muttered, "We'll work together. Just give us another chance."

Hector shook his head. "No one doubts your dedication, but you two are not ready."

Tomas pleaded, "You've got to take us. Give us another test. Anything."

Hector shook his head slowly. "Soldier, the missions we will face don't give second chances. We succeed, or we die. Second chances are like petting a sleeping torc, unlikely at the best of times, and usually fatal."

The captain turned away amid a round of laughter.

Sergeant Rory shook his head again. "Forget about becoming Fast Rollers. Chances of you two making it into this company are about as likely as seeing a torc fly."

That triggered another round of laughter as Rory turned away and led his company back toward the exit. As the others dispersed, followed by a dejected Tomas, Cameron remained rooted in place. He didn't get many ideas, and the unfamiliar feeling of inspiration burning through his mind left him speechless and feeling a little unsteady.

He allowed a slow grin as his feeling of crushing despair from their loss faded under the hint of a new hope that no one but he seemed to have grasped.

"Captain wants a torc."

CHAPTER THREE

CAMERON ACTUALLY GETS A BRILLIANT IDEA. MAYBE.

If anyone had ever suggested that Tomas might dread Boulder training, he would have punched the fool over the central palace. As he trotted out through the huge eastern gate of Merkland's famous white granite wall and headed down the road toward the practice field, he realized with a shock that he was the fool. In the five days since the humiliating failed attempt to join the Fast Rollers, he'd been forced to re-live that failure daily.

It was Cameron's fault.

He spotted his partner waiting among the line of Boulders accepting their daily training portion of powdered granite from a sergeant at the distribution cart on the side of the road. He scowled at nothing in particular. The fifty other Boulders lined up for their portions or scattered across the wide field of close-cropped grass, stretching and preparing for the day's training, all looked happy. Even the beautiful, sunny morning seemed to mock him. The sky was a deep, sapphire blue, pierced by the northern mountains, with nary a cloud visible. It seemed wrong that everything and everyone else seemed perfectly content to move on with life, despite his unthinkable loss.

When he reached the front of the line for his own portion, he asked as he had five times before, "Sergeant, request permission to train with a different partner."

"Denied."

Sergeant Alban didn't bother trying to hide his smile under that huge mustache he was always stroking. The man looked exactly like a Boulder shouldn't. He was tall, with gangly limbs and a skinny neck. How he won the honor of sergeant in charge of Boulder daily practice was a mystery, although Tomas wondered if the mustache had anything to do with it. The man was clearly trying to mimic the famous mustaches of the Grandurian general, Wolfram, but so far they'd only earned Alban the nickname of Stretched Wolf.

"How long are you going to keep up this farce?" Tomas growled as he absorbed the full measure of his daily portion.

"When you and your partner learn to work together, of course," Alban grinned.

With the rush of his curse roaring through his limbs, Tomas was tempted to throw Alban across the training field, or maybe over the palace. He was confident Cameron would happily help him demonstrate to Alban that they could work together long enough to beat him to a pulp.

"He's not my partner," was all he said.

Alban shook his head. "That's not what Captain Hector said. You were officially assigned partners and until new orders are issued, partners you will stay. Now get to it."

Tomas marched away, muttering curses to himself, trying to ignore the snickers of the other Boulders. The company seemed to take far too much pleasure in his failure. Of course, he'd bragged for weeks that he'd easily make the ranks of the Fast Rollers, and no one liked a braggart who couldn't deliver. They seemed to take particular pleasure in asking him if he'd received word of transfer back to Raineach. The thought of returning south as a failure infuriated him even more.

It was Cameron's fault.

"Hey Tomas, where are your chains?" one sallow-faced new recruit called.

That was a new one. Tomas turned and scowled at the man. A week ago, the fellow wouldn't have dared talk to him like that. "I was planning to rip out your guts and use those."

The younger man's smile faded, but his sparring partner, a stocky fellow that Tomas had considered a friend, took up the taunt for him. "Your partner's been running into the woods every evening, carrying enough chains to hang everyone who's ever known him."

"You say he keeps coming back?" Tomas asked.

"Aye, and he brings the chains back too."

Tomas shrugged. "I've said all along he's got nothing but loose rocks rolling around in that skull of his."

The man gave him a disgusted look, as if Cameron's antics were his fault. "He's your partner. Keep him in line."

Tomas didn't bother answering, but stalked onto the practice field, pushing through the lines of men who he had hoped might learn to respect him. Instead of celebrating his failure, they should understand that if he could fail, they had no chance at succeeding.

"About time," Cameron said when Tomas arrived and they began slowly circling, preparing for the one part of the forced partnership that Tomas actually enjoyed. He'd never admit it, but Cameron was a world-class bash fighter.

"So where are your chains?" Tomas asked, throwing an exploratory punch.

Instead of launching into a full-force assault like he usually did, Cameron just side-stepped and continued circling. "Why would I bring chains to a practice session? Have you been smoking carrot juice again?"

"What are you doing with them out in the woods?" Tomas asked.

"None of your business." Cameron finally threw a good punch, but then again side-stepped Tomas's return jab.

"Did that blind woman run you off?" Tomas teased. "Even if you chain a sighted woman down long enough to have dinner together, the sight of your ugly face would probably blind her."

"At least I've got a woman willing to swing a frying pan at my head. What have you got? Merkland women have no use for losers who fail to make the cut in two different realms."

With the insults ringing with better than average tempo, Tomas launched into a focused assault, raining blows upon his partner, eager for a furious bash fight. Cameron obliged, and for a moment they pounded on each other with unrestrained enthusiasm.

All bash fights end too soon, and Cameron ended that one by ducking a blow that he should have taken in the face, spinning Tomas around and pushing him off balance.

"Who taught you to fight, the family goat?"

Tomas regained his footing and tried not to smile. That was a pretty good warm up. "At least I don't train by hitting myself over the head with logs."

"You're so dumb, you haven't even figured out yet that whoever brings the captain that torc will get his second chance."

Tomas was already opening his mouth to throw out his next insult, so it was easy to stop and gape.

Cameron scowled and stepped closer, thrusting a meaty finger into Tomas's face. "That's my secret, so you can't keep it."

"It's not a secret if you're cracked," Tomas scoffed, although a terrible fear began to form in his mind. "Captain never told us to bring him a torc."

Cameron tapped the side of his nose and gave Tomas a sly smile. "You should stop filling your ears with leftover potatoes."

"Captain said there are no second chances," Tomas insisted, blustering to hide his worry. Could Cameron have actually figured out something before him?

"That's not what he said," Cameron retorted. He made a brushing gesture and added, "Forget about it. You believe what captain said. It's easier to accept that you're responsible for making us fail when you don't believe there's anything else you can do."

"It's your fault," Tomas snapped. "You should have thrown me."

"I'll throw you now."

Cameron lunged, and Tomas eagerly tapped more granite and threw himself at his cracked partner. He was expecting the second bashing session to intensify even more than the first, but instead of plowing into Tomas's best punches, Cameron surprised him by dancing around his blows, shifting and ducking and shedding the worst of the hits like a duck shedding rainwater. He still punched hard, but as Tomas paid more attention, he recognized the minute shifting in Cameron's size between blows.

He was constantly changing his tap rate.

Tomas took a step back and glared. "Failing that contest wrecked you, Cameron. You can't even bash fight as good as you used to."

"I don't have to max-tap to beat you," Cameron said a bit defensively.

"What's really going on with you?" Tomas demanded. He'd thought he understood the hard-headed northerners, but Cameron wasn't acting normal, and it didn't make sense.

His brutish partner shrugged. "Sergeant Alban is always saying improving tap-rate management is the key to more advanced fighting."

"Since when has Sergeant Alban said anything useful?"

"You've got a point," Cameron conceded.

"And you've never worried about it before. You're like me. Who cares about tap-rate management when we can beat down any opposition faster than anyone?"

"We didn't beat down those Fast Rollers," Cameron pointed out.

"Reducing tap rate wouldn't have helped. They would've just clobbered us faster."

"I know," Cameron snapped, his frustration plain on his ugly face. "But if we don't try something new, how can we know it's still wrong?"

"Go kiss a pedra. Tell me how well that works."

"I'm not interested in pedras."

Then Tomas understood. "You're trying to save some of your portion for torc hunting, aren't you?"

"Tallan take it," Cameron growled, stepping closer. "Keep your voice down."

"Are you skimming off the duty rounds too?" Tomas demanded.

If Cameron wanted to risk absorbing less than a full training portion and maybe run out of power during a training bout, that was on him, but the portions issued during their duty watches were strictly monitored. They were not to be used except for emergencies, and any shortage in the weight when the portions were turned back in at the end of a shift had to be accounted for. Mishandling power stone was a serious offense, and if Cameron got pounded for such a crime, would it dishonor Tomas by proximity?

Cameron scoffed, "Of course not. I'm not completely daft."

"Could've fooled me."

Cameron barked a laugh. "Anyone could fool you. You still think potatoes grow underground."

Tomas blinked. "They do."

"Ha!" Cameron chortled. "Everyone knows potatoes are like corn. They grow on trees."

"Have you been sniffing the tanner's vats again?" Tomas asked. How could he have ever feared Cameron might actually have a good idea?

But what if he was right about the torc?

"What I do on my own time is none of your business," Cameron said defensively.

"Unless you spend that time hiking the mountains with enough chains to swing over the chasm into Granadure. If you defect, you damage my reputation too."

"You do enough damage to it all on your own," Cameron said. "In a few days, you'll be wishing you were still my partner."

Sergeant Alban whistled loudly, the one talent he seemed to possess besides growing long mustaches. The sound called them to assemble for group drills that would take up the rest of the training session. During the training, Tomas couldn't help thinking about what Cameron had said. The distraction made him perform worse than usual, triggering fresh rounds of jeers, but he barely noticed.

After the training session ended, Tomas watched Cameron trot off the field, convinced his partner was a daft-cracked lunatic chaser.

But what if he was right about that torc?

As he walked alone back to the barracks, he thought again back to the failed challenge match. Everything had gone so well until that final beat down. Maybe they shouldn't have broken so many of the walls in that little shack?

The shame of his failure ate at him. He couldn't wait a year to get his second chance. The risk of getting shipped back to Raineach in shame was too great. He thought back to what Captain Hector had said, trying to piece together the exact words. They had broken and scattered in his mind, so it took a while to collect and assemble them into more or less the right order.

Tomas stopped in the corridor outside the barracks, staring at nothing. The captain had said something about torcs and second chances. Even if Cameron wasn't interpreting the captain's meaning right, Tomas couldn't take that chance.

He had to catch himself a torc, and he had to get one before Cameron.

CHAPTER FOUR

Talking with Women Can Be Inspiring

he next week passed far too quickly for Cameron. He had expected to find a torc the first night, but the deadly creatures were even more crafty than he had heard. It was hard to believe that beasts that could grow as big as an ox could remain concealed in the hills around Merkland. He saw lots of cows and sheep as he hiked the lanes around farm pastures, but nary a sign of a torc.

He worried sometimes about sharing the secret with Tomas, but his partner hadn't mentioned it again, and he dared to hope Tomas had forgotten all about it. He was usually pretty effective at not taxing his mind or his memory, so Cameron made sure to not talk about it again.

After returning the third night in a row with nothing to show for his long journey but aching muscles, he wondered if he needed to try something different. He dropped the long lengths of heavy chain at the quartermaster outpost, feeling dejected.

"No luck again?" asked the plump, middle-aged woman who manned the office. She leaned on the counter, her open face honestly inquisitive. Few women looked at him at all, and most of those who did couldn't hide their distaste at his brutish features. It felt good to meet someone willing to just talk with him.

"Nothing," he admitted, disgusted by the entire process.

"What are you doing every day with those chains anyway?"

Cameron hesitated. It was his great secret, but then again she wasn't a warrior. She couldn't steal his torc and use it to win a second chance from the captain. Besides, she was a woman who wanted to talk with him. He needed all the practice he could get.

"I need to find a torc."

Instead of mocking him like the other Boulders had been doing in recent days, she only nodded gravely. "Torcs are rare. Hard to catch. Especially by someone who's not a hunter."

He nodded. "You'd think they'd be better trained. When a man's got to find one, all this chasing through the hills wastes a lot of time."

The woman's lips twitched into an almost smile. "That's probably why they're called wild animals."

"Not wild enough. They didn't make any noise that I could hear."

"Where have you been looking?"

"All over." Cameron's shoulders and back ached. He hadn't yet saved up enough extra granite powder to tap it just to carry chains around. Even though he was a big guy, he wasn't used to performing such extended manual labor without the help of his curse.

He scratched at the back of his head. He didn't bother wearing a beard. Facial hair never worked for him, and the sparse, scraggly growth he grew only made him look worse. "I think I've circled every farm within ten miles."

"Have you tried hunting up into the mountains? You know, the game trails and those high mountain meadows no one lives in?"

Cameron grimaced. "That sounds like a lot of work."

The woman chuckled. "I've heard torcs don't like people, so it makes sense they'd live farther out, doesn't it?"

"Maybe," he conceded. "How did you hear all that?"

"My husband's brother is a huntsman. He loves to tell stories."

Cameron considered that. The huntsmen usually lacked any affinity with power stones, but the few he'd met were all tough men who could track and stalk and do all those mysterious hunting things that no one else seemed to understand. He was glad he had confided in the woman. He hadn't realized he'd have to strategize his assault on the torc, but maybe that was why the captain suggested he get one. If he could prove he was smarter than a torc, captain would have to give him a second chance, wouldn't he?

The problem he faced was that he would need more time to climb that high into the mountains. His current excursions were already keeping him out until after dark. He had a rare day without a duty assignment coming up in the next week. Maybe he should use the entire day to hunt.

"Those mountains are big. I could hunt for weeks."

"Especially since you don't know where to find them," she agreed. "My relative and the other huntsmen are often gone for days. Have you asked the hunt master for suggestions about where to find your trophy torc?"

"Brilliant," Cameron exclaimed. That was the key piece of idea he needed to make his torc assault work. "I could kiss you."

Her smile vanished. "Nice try son, but you'd have better luck kissing your torc."

"I'd settle for catching one." He bowed to her. "Thank you."

"Good luck," she said as he turned and marched back toward his bunk with a new sense of purpose.

CHAPTER FIVE

THE DANGERS OF TRYING NEW THINGS

omas punched Cameron in the nose, increasing his tap rate in the fraction of a second before the blow struck. He had waited a hair too long and his hand wasn't quite rock solid when it smashed into Cameron's stony face. The stab of pain faded away a heartbeat later though as his skin deadened and became numb under the influence of granite.

Cameron returned with a heavy blow to Tomas's midsection, and Tomas noted the shifting of plates along his partner's arm as Cameron increased the tap rate to his arm. Tomas applied more granite to his stomach and ribs to help absorb the blow. Again he reacted a fraction too slow, and Cameron's fist drove into his slushy-hard stomach, doubling him over and blasting the breath out of his lungs. Cameron's other fist caught Tomas in the chin and the blow knocked him right off his feet.

Tomas lay on his back for a moment, blinking at the morning sun, trying to remember what happened. The two of them had moved to the outer edge of the practice ground outside of the city, and the high, white granite walls gleamed in the sunlight a couple hundred yards to the south.

It was market day, and Merkland was teeming with activity as commoners from outlying farms and towns crowded the streets and haggled loudly. A troup of musicians had begun playing just inside the wall, and their fast, foot-tapping songs echoed across the open fields.

Cameron moved into view, grinning. "You forget to take your portion today?"

Tomas was tempted to max-tap granite and pound that smile off of Cameron's face, but he resisted the urge. He had started reducing how much of his daily training portion he consumed, trying to save as much powder as he could for the torc hunt he was planning in a couple days. He had started hoarding powder later than Cameron, so he needed to save out more each day. What remained wasn't enough for his usual max-tapped brawl.

So he extended a hand, and Cameron actually hauled him to his feet.

"Like you said, we should try something different to prove it's still wrong."

Cameron barked a laugh. "You actually remembered something you heard? Where'd you find a chicken willing to loan you some extra brains?"

"I asked that goat you tried borrowing chin hairs from."

Cameron punched him in the ribs.

Tomas grunted with pain as he again applied the granite too late. He hated bruises, but he was going to have a lot of them if he didn't figure out how to manage his tap rate better.

So he kicked Cameron in the knee.

When his ugly partner yelped and doubled over, he applied maximum granite to his fist and raised it high, pausing for half a second for the curse to harden and deaden the skin, then slammed it down onto the back of Cameron's neck. It was Cameron's turn to collapse to the ground.

"I think we proved this whole tap-rate management thing is nothing but a bucket of Tallan droppings," Tomas said as he hauled Cameron to his feet.

"You're wrong."

They both turned at the unexpected sound of Alban's voice. Usually the sergeant barely took notice of them during training practice. The past days of taunting and forcing them to train together had been the most Tomas had heard from the man in months. He usually spent most of his time working with younger recruits who didn't know how to bash fight yet.

Alban faced them, arms crossed, expression curious. "I usually hate admitting when I'm wrong, but I would have sworn you two would never amount to anything but max-tapped bash fighters."

Tomas shrugged. "No need to apologize." He liked being a max-tapped bash fighter.

"I'm impressed," Alban continued. "Most men in your position would have done little more than wallow in their failure and pick fights with everyone teasing them."

Tomas exchanged a glance with Cameron who said, "Figured to start them next week."

"You're not fooling me," Alban chided, and Tomas felt his hope crash into a burning pile in his boots. Alban had noticed them hoarding powder. He hadn't realized that was against regulations, but no doubt it was.

"I can explain," Cameron blurted out before Tomas could.

"You don't have to," Alban said, but he was smiling instead of wearing that totally unintimidating look he usually assumed when preparing to reprimand soldiers under his command.

"All right," Cameron said with a shrug. "Takes less energy that way."

"Exactly," Alban said, his smile widening. "So few Boulders ever understand. I hadn't thought you two would figure it out."

The gangly sergeant was making even less sense than usual.

Tomas wondered if he'd overworked his brain muscles the day before and they'd shut down to recuperate. "We're a lot smarter than most of us usually think."

"I'm starting to believe it," Alban said. "But you should have come to me before trying to practice advanced tap-rate management drills. You haven't been trained properly, and you're making mistakes that I can help you avoid."

"What kind of mistakes?" Tomas asked, relieved that the sergeant was misinterpreting their powder hoarding for an attempt to learn something.

"You can't just drop your tap-rate to zero, at least not yet. You don't have the timing down to apply your curse where it's needed in time to avoid damage."

"But if we keep the burn high, we'll still exhaust our powder as fast as always," Cameron protested.

"I didn't say keep it high," Alban said. "You're Boulders, so when you go into a fight, you need to apply your curse to your entire bodies. To do otherwise is foolish. The trick is to keep the burn really low, barely engaged. That way you burn through your powder stores at one tenth the rate, but your curse is already engaged, making it far easier and faster to increase the tap rate and apply your strength when you need it."

Tomas frowned as he considered that. Remarkably, the idea actually made sense. He grunted, "You'd better be careful, sergeant, or someone might start rumors that you've got things to teach the rest of us."

Alban's expression turned long-suffering. "Focus. You will duel me first."

Tomas grinned. He'd been looking for an excuse to hit Alban for a long time.

"When do I get to beat you up?" Cameron asked.

"Your turn is coming," Alban said, squaring off with Tomas. The sergeant wore battle leathers like the rest of them, but they looked ridiculous on the gangly man. Tomas noted a subtle shifting of plates and creaking of leather as Alban tapped his curse.

"Remember, keep the burn to minimum, but applied everywhere," Alban directed.

Tomas embraced his curse, a process as familiar to him as breathing. Applying it to his entire body came easier than eating with utensils, and his battle leathers creaked as his muscles expanded.

Reducing the tap rate to the bare minimum proved harder than he expected. He rarely tapped his curse without drawing deeply from it. Why bother drawing upon the power to smash through stone walls and shatter pumpkins with his face only to not use as much as possible.

Alban watched the expanding then contracting of Tomas's battle plates with approval. Without warning, he punched Tomas in the stomach. He probably thought the move would surprise Tomas, but he broadcast the hit early, and he moved far slower than Cameron. Tomas instinctively increased the burn of his curse in his midsection, hardening the muscles and deadening the skin in plenty of time before the blow struck.

"Good," Alban said. "Did you notice how much easier it was to adjust the tap rate when you already had the active burn?"

Tomas nodded and decided it was only polite to punch Alban in the stomach in turn.

Alban's torso hardened, his skin fading even as the blow struck. It didn't help. He might be fast at tapping his curse, but his balance was off, and the punch catapulted him off his feet. He tumbled right through three other pairs of dueling Boulders, scattering soldiers like crows before a pedra and sliding face down for thirty feet along the hard-packed soil, leaving a little furrow where his teeth dug in.

"He's a better teacher than I expected," Tomas said.

"I can't wait for my chance to do that to him," Cameron laughed.

"It might be a few minutes. Looks like he swallowed a lot of dirt. I'll teach you what I learned."

He punched Cameron in the face.

The resulting bash fight was a joy. Holding the low burn did make it easier to adjust his focused power to the muscles that needed it the most. Cameron caught on quickly, and the two of them beat on each other with almost as much fury as normal, but burned through only half as much powder.

"This is great," Cameron said when Sergeant Alban's whistle rang across the field. It sounded a bit shaky, and his face still looked pale as the company formed up for group training.

Tomas was glad they hadn't waited for him to recover. He might have things still to teach, but Tomas was starting to suspect Alban might not be able to handle more than one good punch a day. "I could beat on you all day with one portion now."

"I can go as long as you, flatlander," Cameron said, raising his fists in an offer to keep fighting.

"Sure. Let's use the rest of our portions after group training."

The group drills and mock battle seemed to take forever, and felt like a waste of time to Tomas since it was preventing him from more bashing time with Cameron. When training finally ended, the two of them beat on each other to a growing crowd of appreciative townsfolk for a full fifteen minutes before Tomas's reduced portion ran out.

"Alban's got smarts," Cameron commented as they headed back into Merkland, the crowds parting for them. "Most days, I nearly ran out of powder by the end of practice, even when using a full measure."

Tomas felt a little disappointed that he actually agreed completely with his partner. That deflated his ability to respond with a proper insult.

When they reached the barracks, Cameron hurried off without even a final glare. He seemed motivated, and moved with purpose. As Tomas watched him go, he was tempted to follow him on his daily hunting trek into the mountains, but couldn't bear the thought of admitting Cameron was right. Not twice in less than an hour. In three days they both had a rare duty-free day. Only the Tallan's own fury would prevent Cameron from spending the day hunting that torc.

Tomas headed for the wash room, making his own plans. If Cameron was going hunting, then so was he. He had dated a butcher's daughter for a time and she had said once that the best torcs came from the north face of Inverey Peak. It was the highest mountain in the range of craggy hills north of Merkland that made up the border with Granadure.

That's where he'd find his torc. Let Cameron hunt the mountains for another week. Tomas would already have won his second chance, and surely Sergeant Rory would assign him a more worthy partner.

CHAPTER SIX

MARCHING ORDERS

ergeant Rory entered Captain Hector's office with a sense of anticipation. The summons had not been expected, and he hoped that meant the Fast Rollers had received a new mission. The office was simple and tidy, with a standard captain's wooden desk and padded wooden chair. Captain Hector had added an overstuffed chair near the small fireplace, two framed pictures of himself on the mantel, and a tall, standing mirror.

"Close the door, Sergeant," Hector said from behind the desk where he was reviewing a piece of parchment. He waved Rory to one of two hard-backed, wooden chairs facing the desk.

"How is training proceeding with the new recruits?" Hector asked.

"Good. They're motivated, and they're picking up the advanced battle tactics quickly. I am confident the entire squad will be ready to join the rest of the company soon."

The five partnerships who had passed the second round culling were all top warriors, and they were taking to the training with enthusiasm. They were exactly the kind of men that Rory had longed to command. His position with the Fast Rollers was the culmination of his entire career, and he felt eager to prove himself and his men.

"Perhaps sooner than you think," Hector said with a smile.

"Sir?" Rory asked, unable to keep a hint of eagerness from his voice.

Hector waved the parchment in his hand. "Scouts have reported movement in the Grandurian mountains close to the border chasm. Possible sighting of Wolfram."

Rory frowned. "Why would he skulk around in that wilderness?"

"That's what we've been ordered to find out."

It was a new mission. Rory allowed a smile. His team was ready.

Hector rose and paced to the fireplace. He stared at the painting of himself in his favorite battle leathers for a moment before turning. "I will take the main company of Fast Rollers north toward the Crask redoubt. That's the most likely position for Wolfram to be operating from."

Rory nodded. "Makes sense."

"But it's not the only possibility," Hector said. "You will take the new recruits to scout the Kinbrace outpost."

That wasn't exactly what Rory had hoped to hear. "There's no evidence that anyone's actually used that outpost in the past two years."

He wouldn't outright argue with his captain, and he was thrilled with the prospect of independently leading his own strike team, but it sounded like Hector was sending him on a wild eoin hunt. He probably saw it as a way to further test the new recruits without placing them in much real danger.

"True," Hector conceded. "But Wolfram is no fool. I must assume he knows he's been spied upon. If I find him at Crask, I will assess the situation and decide if it warrants an attack." He allowed a predatory grin. "Maybe I'll get a chance to take that Tallan-cursed wolf in his lair."

That would be an amazing coup. Wolfram was perhaps the most wily and resourceful Grandurian commander. Although the two countries were technically at peace, they sparred constantly across the border, testing each other's defenses and maneuvering for potential advantage. If Wolfram was exploring the wilderness along the chasm, it might be in preparation for a more substantial raid into Obrion.

"Intelligence suggests he's not preparing a major incursion," Hector said, as if reading Rory's thoughts. "But it is possible."

"Does the report suggest what he might be doing out there?"

"Not directly, but I've seen a couple reports recently that suggest the Grandurians may be exploring a potential new site of power-grade stone along the border."

Rory whistled softly. "That would be worth the risk." A new source of stone and right on the border posed a real threat and a potentially huge advantage.

Hector nodded. "If we can find out the truth of those reports, we could tip the balance of power along the border in our favor."

"Would High Lord Dougal approve invasion?" Rory asked, both thrilled and a bit nervous by the idea. Such a move could trigger an escalation of hostilities greater than they'd seen in a generation. Rory and his men were ready for anything, but as he considered the readiness of Dougal's other forces, he wasn't sure they were best positioned for such an escalation.

Hector shrugged. "I leave the politics to the high lords, but the tactical situation might justify it. If a new supply of power stone lies close to the border, we wouldn't need to take much to win great advantage. The terrain is

48

difficult to reach, so it would be hard for Granadure to launch an effective counter-attack."

"So if my squad finds Kinbrace garrisoned," Rory said, turning his thoughts to the upcoming mission.

"Your orders are to gather intelligence. Do not initiate hostilities. We cannot risk giving Wolfram the excuse to reinforce his border fortifications before we're ready to move."

The orders made sense, which was not always a requirement for their missions. Rory would have preferred authorization to strike if the situation appeared advantageous.

Hector continued. "Gregor will create the crossing for us, and he will accompany me toward Crask. Garvin will provide the tertiary support for your squad."

Rory nodded. He would have preferred another Sentry, especially in the mountains. There was no matching the earth movers for effectiveness if conflict became unavoidable. Since their mission called for stealth, a Spitter might be a better choice than a Firetongue, but Garvin wasn't as bad as many of the wild fire chewers Rory had met.

"When do we leave?" Rory asked.

"Three days. Make sure your men are ready."

CHAPTER SEVEN

FULL CONTACT TORC HUNTING

ameron trotted up a steep, rocky goat path leading from the last farmer's paddock and into the uncultivated hills north of Merkland. He had never ventured so far from the city except when on patrol, and he felt excited to see what lay over the first row of hills. The last village lay three miles back down the valley, so he was entering the wilds where torcs were surely easy to find.

He maintained a low tap rate as he climbed, and the gentle itching of his curse bolstered his confidence while strengthening his muscles against the strain of carrying the heavy chains up the slope. In the past few days since he'd spoken with the brilliant quartermaster, he'd saved his daily portions even more aggressively.

The training with Alban had helped more than he had imagined, although he still felt a bit cheated that he hadn't gotten to punch the gangly sergeant. Even so, he had saved enough powder to dare tap some to assist his incursion into the mountain.

The jagged summit of Inverey Peak loomed to the northeast. The track he was following was supposed to eventually skirt its western flank. The chasm marking the border with Granadure cut the mountains just north of the peak. He had patrolled that area several times along established roads in his Boulder company, but had never attempted to penetrate the mountains alone.

He doubted he would have to go that far. He had finally tracked down the hunt master the night before, and the man had offered exactly the intelligence he had hoped for.

The bearded, tanned hunt master, whose piercing blue eyes reminded Cameron of a hawk's, had slapped his thigh and chuckled when Cameron explained what he was looking for.

"By Tallan's gouted wind, that's a first, master Cameron, that is," he'd chuckled. "I've hunted torcs for decades, and they're as fine a trophy as any man can hope to take, but I'll be grouted and served as chink mud if I've ever heard anyone try to capture one of the beasts and drag it back to Merkland in chains, no less."

"Captain wants a torc," Cameron explained with a shrug.

"Then by the Tallan's tainted glory, he should have one," the hunt master had agreed with a grave nod. He had explained that Cameron's best chance at finding a trophy torc was to skirt Inverey Peak and hunt the high meadows at the edge of the border chasm.

"They're solitary animals, are torcs," the hunt master had said. "You've got the strength of granite on your side, but I've seen torcs taken by a fury of the high mountains, I have. Tis a frightful thing, a torc in a killin' fury. So you take it fast and bind it well, master Cameron, or it'll have you for dinner."

"Captain's the one looking for dinner," Cameron assured him. "Don't fret yourself, master hunter. I'll win my second chance, mark my words."

The hunt master had laughed again and slapped his thigh for emphasis. "Second chance. Good name for a chained torc, I say. Good luck."

Cameron paused at the crest of the steep slope to scan the first of the high meadows. He was still a little south of Inverey Peak, but there was no reason not to hope a torc had come a little farther south to feed. He spotted a pair of mountain deer, but saw no torcs. He did catch a flash of movement from the rocks above the meadow that might have been a nuall. The large hunting cats blended well with the grays and browns of the slope, so they were hard to spot.

The sun was still only halfway down to the western horizon, and the hunt master had cautioned Cameron that the best time to find a torc would be late afternoon into evening. He still had time to reach prime hunting ground, so Cameron shrugged the heavy lengths of chain to a more comfortable position and trotted onward. He'd easily reach the north face of Inverey Peak in time.

Or maybe not.

Distances in the mountains turned out to be deceptive. He wasn't sure if the thinner air made the sweeping vistas arrive quicker, but Inverey turned out to be a lot farther away than it looked. The sun seemed to accelerate down toward the line of hills to the west as he jogged through the afternoon, as if eager to end the hunt before it really began and mock him with yet another failure. Cameron tapped more of his precious powder and broke into a run.

"Tallan's blasted bald knees, I will find a torc," Cameron growled as he charged across grassy meadows and scrambled along shifting slopes of scree. One misstep could send him tumbling down deep ravines that he might never climb back out of, but he ignored the danger and pounded on.

For another half an hour he raced the setting sun before he topped a long, gradual slope of scraggly trees and sparse mountain grasses and finally reached the southwest flank of Inverey Peak. Breathing hard from the mountain run, he slowed to cross yet another steep slope covered in broken stone from a recent slide. The delay only made him more determined than ever to find a beast for the captain.

Captain Hector had better be overjoyed by the torc when Cameron finally got it back to Merkland, or he'd beat the captain with it.

He found an animal trail on the far side of the rock slide and began weaving up through another wild meadow, dotted with high bushes, tangles of trees, and piles of black volcanic rock. It wasn't power stone, so he didn't really care enough to identify it. This meadow seemed more lush than previous ones, as if the steep hills rearing to either side had squeezed the remaining meadowland and condensed it. Shadows hung heavy in the air as they crept from their daytime hiding places, and the air began to cool. The meadow smelled of clover and pine and dusty stone.

Then Cameron heard it.

Somewhere not far ahead, around a jumbled pile of rocks flanked by a stand of what he thought might be alder trees, something made a coughing, wheezing sound and a series of low growling, huffing noises. It sounded nothing like a deer, an ox, or even a dog. It had to be a torc.

Cameron slowed and carefully unwound the chain from his shoulders. His fingers tingled with the same thrill he felt just before leaping into a bash fight, and he grinned as he crept forward, trying to be as careful as possible. Sergeant Rory would be proud of his sneakifying skills.

A deep, huffing grunt echoed down the meadow and Cameron's excitement grew. That sounded exactly like what he'd imagined a torc should. It was as if the torc had swallowed a pack of wolf hounds and they were all growling together. Tapping more granite, Cameron broke into a sprint and rushed around the last jumble of rocks, chains poised to throw.

There! Standing in the shadows of the rocks, barely twenty feet ahead, a large shape turned to face him. The slope leveled out into a sizable clearing in that area, a perfect place to meet the monster.

It really was a torc. The majestic creature was fully as big as an ox, but was built low to the ground like a boar. Its massive head was long and blocky, with a thick horn protruding from the center of its armored forehead. Sharp tusks curved out low to either side of its wide, flat mouth. When it spotted him, it slashed at nearby bushes with those tusks and pawed the rocky ground with a sharply cloven hoof.

Cameron grinned, delighted with the impressive specimen. "Just what the captain ordered."

The torc huffed again, louder than before, and the sharp report held a note of warning.

"I'm not a huntsman you can scare away," Cameron said as he stalked toward the beast. "You can come quiet, or I'll deliver you with all that pretty armor dented, but you will come."

Its long, powerful body was covered in thick, gray hide with wide slabs of stony armor protecting its shoulders and back, lending it the impression of a fully armored knight. Fighting such a beast would be a wonderful challenge. It bellowed again and charged.

Tapping granite, Cameron rushed to meet it. Bash fighting a torc was exactly how he had hoped the hunt would end. As he rushed to meet the charging beast, he felt ready for anything.

He hadn't expected a huge rock to fly out of the darkening sky and clobber him in the side of the head.

The unexpected blow toppled him from his feet, and the torc thundered past, shaking the ground with its passage. He had been tapping granite, so the brutal impact didn't really hurt, but he raged at the sight of his torc getting away. He sat up, wondering if the mountain had decided to avalanche.

An exuberant battle cry rang through the valley. Tomas leaped off a nearby pile of stones and landed right on the back of the startled torc.

CHAPTER EIGHT

GREATER STRENGTH SOMETIMES ONLY MAKES GREATER PROBLEMS

Tomas laughed as he landed on the huge torc's back. Throwing that rock at Cameron had been a brilliant idea. He'd hiked all afternoon and spotted Cameron half an hour ago. Sergeant Rory would be proud of his stalkifying skills. Cameron had never seen him, had never expected to get attacked in his moment of glory.

That kind of mistake was about to cost Cameron his second chance. Tomas was already reaching for the long, heavy rope coiled over one shoulder to tie the torc before it could recover from his surprise attack. He expected to knock the monster right off its feet with his surprise tackle.

The torc did not fall. The impact rocked the creature, but it did little more than stumble. It stood perfectly still for a single heartbeat, as if trying to accept the fact that it now bore a human rider.

Then it erupted into a frenzy, bucking and leaping, twisting and bellowing like a thousand cats had all gotten their tails stomped at the same time. Tomas tried clinging to the bony, armored plating of its back, but couldn't get a secure enough hold. He barely lasted three seconds before tumbling off the torc's back and crashing through a couple nearby trees.

The torc came after him, its bellowing roar like a thunderclap that echoed back and forth across the steep hills flanking the flat, narrow meadow. Just as Tomas heaved himself back to his feet, the torc plowed into him, spearing his midsection with its deadly horn.

Tomas was already tapping granite, and only his recent training in managing his tap rate saved him from getting gored. He max-tapped granite to his midsection an eyeblink before the horn punched through his armor.

So great was the torc's weight and momentum that the horn stabbed an inch into his stone-hard skin. Tomas shouted with pain and the thrill of battle as the beast continued its charge, driving him through the rest of the stand of small trees, snapping trunks and trampling smaller saplings. As it drove him through the grove, the impacts pressed him back against it, his torso draped over the torc's head, his legs dragging on the ground just inside the curve of those deadly tusks. Its thick hide was covered sparsely in black hairs that stabbed into his face, and its heavy, musky scent clung to his mouth and nostrils.

"Get off," Tomas shouted, punching the torc in the eye.

The beast shook its head, throwing Tomas several yards. He bounced off a thicker tree, rolled with the impact, and came to his feet to face the huge brute.

"That's my torc!" Cameron shouted as he charged through the wreckage of the grove after them.

The beast spun to meet him, bellowed another angry cry, and charged.

Cameron was ready for it. He sidestepped the torc and punched it in the side of its massive jaw. The blow drove its head up and sideways, pulling its front legs right off the ground and sending it into a spinning dive.

Cameron jumped on it before it finished sliding through the grass and leaves, whipping heavy lengths of chain around its thrashing legs. He would have the torc trussed like a sogail eoin roast in seconds.

So Tomas ripped the nearest tree out by the roots and used it like a club to knock Cameron flying.

"I tackled it first," he shouted as he tried pulling his rope from his shoulder. The long lengths of heavy line had gotten tangled in his wild plunge through the trees, and the more he tugged on them, the worse they bunched around his shoulders. In seconds, he had tied himself up so tight, he could barely move, even tapping granite.

Cameron came back to his feet in a rush. "I found it."

"But you forgot to watch for a counter attack," Tomas reminded him, smiling as he remembered the image of that rock bouncing off Cameron's thick skull. The look of absolute surprise on his face was already a precious memory.

"Torcs don't counter attack."

The beast lunged back to its feet, shedding Cameron's chains. Tomas expected it to charge one of them and he silently urged it to pick him. He wouldn't make the same mistake and let it get the best of him again.

"Come on," Cameron yelled, gesturing the creature to attack him.

"Over here!" Tomas yelled.

Cameron charged it, so Tomas did too. If Cameron wanted to fight over the prize, he would be happy to oblige.

The torc swung its huge head from Cameron to Tomas, and Tomas grinned. It somehow knew it should surrender to him.

Instead of charging him, the torc wheeled and fled, galloping up the steep meadow with remarkable speed.

Tomas stopped beside Cameron and they exchanged a surprised look.

"Hey," Cameron shouted after the creature. "Where are you going?"

"Think captain will care that we got him a cowardly torc?"

"I won't tell him if you don't."

"Good. Then when I present the prize to him, I'll put in a good word for you."

"It's my prize," Cameron said, breaking into a run and shouting, "Get back here, torc!"

Tomas gave chase. The sun had already slipped behind the western hills and twilight wouldn't last much longer. They had to run that beast to ground before full dark or it might slip away.

It wouldn't escape. There was no way a big monster like that could outrun the two of them.

Tomas realized within the first ten seconds that he was completely wrong. He and Cameron ran up the slope with granite-enhanced legs that threw them ten feet with every leaping stride, but the torc moved twice as fast. It raced up the meadow and tore across the face of a steep slope on a track so narrow its armored shoulder scraped the rock on the uphill side.

"It's getting away," Cameron growled between panting breaths.

"We need to think smarter," Tomas said, even though he was usually the first to warn bash fighters not to try fighting and thinking at the same time. It was too easy to get confused.

He spotted a rock the size of Cameron's fat head, swept it off the ground, and threw it with all his enhanced strength. The torc was getting pretty far ahead and he wouldn't get another chance.

The rock drilled through the darkening twilight, shot across the slope after the torc, and smashed into the monster's hind legs. The impact swept its rear hooves off the narrow path, and the torc squealed like a pig as it lost its footing and slid rear-first down the slope.

"Tallan take it and grind it for porridge," Cameron growled as the two of them reached the slope and looked down. The torc was sliding toward the edge of a near-vertical chasm that ran northeast to southwest, cutting through the rugged mountains like a dark snake.

They had traveled farther north than Tomas had realized and his heart sank as he watched the torc near the drop-off.

"That's the border chasm," Cameron said. "If it falls in there, we'll have to start all over again and find another one."

"It won't fall," Tomas assured him, pointing. The torc had finally stopped sliding. At the lowest end of the slope, just before the edge of the border chasm, it reached a narrow shelf that skirted the edge and gave it enough purchase to regain its footing.

"Where is it going now?" Cameron muttered as the torc began trotting northeast along the lip of the chasm. Within seconds, it rounded a shoulder of rock and disappeared from view.

"Let's find out." Tomas stepped off the trail, increased his tap rate, and began sliding down the slope. His battle leathers protected him from the worst of the scraping, so he only had to apply his precious granite stores to his hands, which he used to steer and control his rapid descent. Cameron followed a couple seconds later.

The air felt noticeably colder in the deeper shadows of the slide as Tomas slid over two hundred yards down the hill. Full night was drawing quickly over the mountains, but bright stars were already visible, sprinkled across the sky in a thickening silver carpet. Tomas wasn't sure how they were going to climb back up to the path they had followed to Inverey Peak, but he decided not to worry about it. He had stood on the edge of the border chasm while on patrol, so he knew at some point an established trail wound all the way down to the lip. Maybe that was where the torc was going.

All he had to worry about was catching that torc.

He hit the flat shelf at the edge of the steep drop-off and breathed a sigh of relief that he hadn't gone over. The chasm was a steep-sided canyon that plunged several hundred feet into darkness in near-vertical cliffs. A constant wind moaned through it, as if despairing its inability to escape the pit. The opposite cliff was closer than he'd expected, barely fifty yards away, and the sound of rushing water echoed off the cliffs. He'd seen glimpses of a fast-flowing river a few times while patrolling, although the chasm had always been wider in the places he'd seen it from the road.

The shelf that bordered the chasm had looked plenty big enough when he had started the descent. There in the gathering darkness deep in the ravine, it seemed miraculous that the torc hadn't bounced right over the edge and plunged into the enormous crack that separated the nations. It was like the mountains on either side shared the same hatred as their peoples and didn't want to even touch at the meeting point.

Cameron landed hard on the shelf beside him with a grunt and peered over the edge for a moment. "Climbing out of that would be harder than stealing a kiss a high lady."

Tomas nodded. "I doubt a high lady would let you get any closer than we are from the bottom."

"You have anything like this down in the flatlands?" Cameron asked, a smug look of superiority on his face that Tomas found supremely annoying.

So he snapped, "Of course not. The north country up here is amazing. Why do you think I'm fighting so hard to stay?"

Cameron looked surprised, and Tomas wished he hadn't shared so much. They might be partners, but it wasn't like they were friends.

Instead of teasing him like Tomas expected, Cameron glanced over the long drop again and asked, "What kind of quarried you got down around Raineach?"

He actually sounded honestly curious. Maybe the higher elevation was addling his brain. "Nothing right near Raineach. It's a processing center where they bring in the stones from outlying areas. The nearest quarries are on the western slopes, near the border with Ravinder. Sandstone."

Cameron grimaced but said, "Healers have their place, mind you, but I'm not sure I could handle living so far from solid granite."

"We have almost as many Striders as Boulders," Tomas admitted. In most realms, the high lords ensured at least a two-to-one majority of Boulders, but the scarcity of granite in Raineach couldn't be so easily overcome.

"That explains it," Cameron said with a satisfied nod. "With fewer Boulders, you have to fight harder to make up the difference. Never made sense before how a soft flatlander could be such a good bash fighter."

That almost sounded like a compliment. Maybe standing so close to the long drop into the black depths of the chasm scared Cameron more than Tomas thought. It was his duty as partner to help Cameron return to more familiar territory.

So he grunted and said, "If you weren't so flabby, maybe you could keep up better."

Cameron looked relieved and barked a laugh. "If I'm flabby, you must stuff your leathers with pillows."

Tomas chuckled in turn, spat over the edge and said, "Let's get that torc."

He turned and began trotting north along the lip of the chasm. After rounding the shoulder of stone, the flat shelf widened into a modest trail and he breathed a little easier. He could still fall off easily enough, but didn't need to fear that any step could be his last.

He glanced back at Cameron. If his partner wanted to remove him from the competition for the torc, he could easily push Tomas over the edge.

"Don't get any stupid ideas," Cameron growled, noting his glance. "Well, nothing stupider than normal. This isn't the place to prove that torc is mine."

"Let's catch it first," Tomas agreed. "Then we'll see who's gone soft."

"I'm more afraid of my blind girlfriend's frying pan than you."

Tomas focused on his footing in the darkness and quickened his pace. Cameron might have a valid point. That blind, frying pan wielding girl was perhaps Cameron's best

66

chance of ever getting a woman. He should be afraid of her. If she turned him down, he might have to take a commission down in Raineach to find another eligible blind girl to take her place.

They trotted in silence for at least a quarter mile as the chasm slowly curved around the flank of Inverey Peak toward the east. They heard nothing but the steady keening of the wind and the constant roar of distant waters in the chasm. Shadows obscured any sign of the torc's passage, but the slope remained steep and impassable on their right so it couldn't have gone any other way.

Thankfully the path they followed along the lip of the chasm continued to slowly widen. Eventually they were trotting along a shelf nearly wide enough to be called a lane. After a few minutes of steady jogging, Tomas began to hear distant echoes of its growling grunts as it trotted ahead of them. The sound encouraged him, and he spent some time untangling the rope still knotted around his shoulders. He wouldn't miss his chance to tie up that beast again.

Eventually Cameron muttered, "Where's it going? You'd think it would've stopped by now."

"Probably hears you. You're not exactly sneakish."

"Neither are you."

"You never heard me closing on you up in that meadow," Tomas pointed out.

Cameron's only reply was a muttered curse and something about pedras in the bloodline. Tomas didn't bother replying. They couldn't afford to get into another bash fight, and he didn't want to make any more noise.

After another ten minutes, they rounded yet another rocky outcrop. The chasm was even narrower there, barely twenty yards across. It seemed amazing that the two countries could draw so close together. Tomas looked around as he passed the obstructing rocks, and stopped so abruptly that Cameron walked right into his back.

The torc had stopped running. The ever-present slope to their right had flattened into a hidden meadow, carpeted with clover and the hardy scrub brush that grew everywhere on the mountain. The torc was grazing in the center of the meadow.

As they stepped off the rocky shelf and into the clearing, its enormous head lifted and swiveled in their direction. Cameron cracked his knuckles loudly, and the torc trumpeted an angry cry and charged.

"Bout time," Tomas grinned and ran to meet the huge beast. His rope was still hopelessly tangled around his shoulders so he called, "I'll distract him. You chain him."

"Told you it was my torc," Cameron said with a loud clinking of chain.

"We can fight over it once we tie it," Tomas replied as he tapped granite.

The torc seemed eager to fight and it centered its horn on his stomach again as it tore across the meadow toward him. Tomas was ready this time and he easily side-stepped the monster. As it thundered past, he punched it in the ribs.

The torc toppled over and crashed to the hard ground with another squealing bellow. Cameron leaped upon it, casting lengths of chain around its thick neck and front legs.

He didn't move fast enough. The torc lunged back to its feet and swung its deadly tusks, catching Cameron in the hip. The sharp tusk slashed through his battle leathers and scraped across his stone-hard skin with a loud rasping sound. The impact threw Cameron from his feet.

"Flabby," Tomas muttered, then lunged, snatched up one end of the chain and whipped it around the torc's front legs. He yanked hard, but only managed to pull one cloven hoof off the ground. The torc spun on three legs and made an ungainly, shuffling lunge to spear Tomas with that annoying horn. He wasn't set properly and when he tried to jump aside, he slipped and fell.

The torc took the chance to bolt again.

"Not this time," Tomas shouted, leaping back to his feet as the beast galloped away. He braced his feet, max-tapping granite. Cameron reached him a second later and together they yanked on the thick chain with all their granite-powered might.

Running at full speed, the torc reached the end of the chain as it swerved closer to the chasm to pass a thick clump of bushes. The chain snapped taut and whipped the torc's head up into the air. Its body followed and it soared off its feet, flying right out over the chasm.

"Pull!" Tomas shouted, and the two of them hauled even harder on the rope. The torc accelerated over the chasm, starting to spin as the chain began unraveling from around its bulk.

"No!" Cameron shouted in helpless frustration as the last length of chain came free and the torc somersaulted away into the darkness.

Tomas rushed to the edge of the chasm and peered into the shadows. The torc looked like a tumbling black mass in the darkness, and his heart sank. They had lost it to the border, and now all their work was wasted. They had to start the hunt all over again.

The tumbling torc bellowed, but the sound cut off abruptly, replaced by the sound of grunting and the crashing of branches.

"It landed on the far side," Cameron exulted.

Tomas nodded. It really did sound like the torc was bouncing through a bunch of bushes. He leaned over the precipice, squinting into the darkness, but a thin screen of clouds had drifted in to obscure the stars, and for a moment he couldn't make out anything clearly.

"The chasm's pretty narrow here, but we need to be sure."

"There!" Cameron cried, and Tomas saw it too a second later.

The thin cloud cover parted, allowing the full radiance of the stars and the new-risen moon to push back the shadows a bit more. The torc was standing on the far side of the chasm, shaking itself free of wood and brush debris. It had fallen into a Grandurian meadow a little lower in elevation than where Tomas and Cameron stood. It appeared to be unhurt.

"Rugged creatures," Tomas commented. He'd participated in a cow throwing contest during the Raineach autumn festival, but those animals were all freshly killed. They were butchered immediately after the throw and served as part of the festival. Those softer cow bodies had always looked battered after the competition, and the steaks had always tasted unusually tender.

Cameron grinned. "Captain'll be thrilled. Now we've got ourselves a Grandurian torc!"

CHAPTER NINE

THE EASY PATH IS NOT ALWAYS EASY

Cameron paced the edge of the chasm, peering vainly into the darkness at the Grandurian slope where the torc had disappeared. It seemed amazing that the land of their enemies came so close he could almost jump across and touch it.

Tomas folded his arms and scowled. "It's gone, Cameron. There's no way across."

He scowled at his partner. "If you hadn't interrupted my hunt, this wouldn't have happened."

"I had it under control," Tomas retorted. "It wasn't until you grabbed the chain too that we sent it tumbling over the chasm."

The chain!

Cameron rushed over to the heavy chain lying forgotten on the ground nearby and snatched up the end. "This is our way across. You can throw me with it."

"You do realize it's not long enough to reach the other side, right?" Tomas asked, still looking like he wanted to wallow in his frustration over losing the torc.

"It's long enough to send me across."

"But that leaves me stranded over here."

"I don't need you to capture my torc."

"And I suppose you have a brilliant plan for getting it back across?"

"I'll figure it out," Cameron insisted. He didn't want to think that far ahead yet. One had to pace themselves between brilliant thoughts to avoid overtaxing brain muscles.

Tomas snorted. "You can barely figure out how to escape your blankets in the morning."

Cameron opened his mouth to fire off a return insult, but the ground began rumbling underfoot. He hated to interrupt the argument before it really got rolling, but standing right there at the edge of the precipice was not a great spot if an earthquake decided to trigger a rockslide.

So he retreated from the edge and cocked his head to listen. The rumbling continued, but did not escalate into the crashing roar of falling stone. Nor did the shaking of the ground grow worse.

"Sounds like Sentry work," Tomas said, glancing around with a frown.

"What would an earth mover be doing out here in the middle of the night?"

"Maybe they heard there's good torc hunting out here."

The sound seemed to be coming from the east, around the next bend in the trail. Cameron moved in that direction, careful to stay on solid rock. As he reached the corner, he scrambled up a pile of jumbled rocks with Tomas close on his heels. After climbing about fifty feet up the slope, they reached a vantage where they could peer around the corner.

A large group of armored men were moving in formation higher up the slope. They weren't walking, but were sliding down the steep slope toward the lip of the chasm, moving at a controlled pace down the slope in a way that only a Sentry could manage. The group was carrying several torches, clearly illuminating Captain Hector and the huge form of Gregor the Sentry at the front of the company.

"Fast Rollers," Tomas breathed as the two of them crouched lower in the shadows.

He was right. Cameron recognized many of them as he scanned the company. He spotted Sergeant Rory near the back, at the head of the five pairs of recent recruits who had passed the second round testing.

His gaze returned to Gregor as the company slid closer, aiming for a spot barely a hundred feet east of where the two of them crouched. Gregor had been a legend since before Cameron was born. Some people whispered that sometimes Gregor seemed to be able to walk with solid stone and not just simple earth, but that was foolish talk. If he hadn't located them before they moved onto solid stone, they would remain invisible to even his earth senses.

"We need to retreat," Tomas whispered, taking a cautions step back. "If they come this way, we're grouted."

Cameron grabbed his arm and pulled him to a stop. He hated to make any sound, but forced himself to whisper, "And if you step onto loose earth, Gregor will sense you in a heartbeat."

The situation could easily turn embarrassing for them. He and Tomas were on a free day, and there was no rule that specifically barred them from hiking along the border at night, but he didn't want to explain to the captain that they'd hunted their second chance all the way to the border gorge, only to lose it to Granadure.

As the company flowed down the slope, the torchlight clearly showed how the earth gripped their boots, holding them secure on the steep grade. Not even a pile of jumbled boulders that perched on the slope, looking like all they needed was an excuse to start an avalanche, slowed their progress. They just slid around the obstruction without slowing. Within seconds, they reached the flat shelf at the lip of the chasm.

Cameron glanced up the slope from where the company had come. No doubt the road he had patrolled a few times passed that spot. It was good to know they were so close to a good road. It would help the return journey.

"What are they doing out here?" Tomas whispered.

"Captain must be incursioning into Granadure."

Sure enough, Captain Hector was already gesturing toward the drop off. The chasm was a little wider there, nearly forty yards. Earth sprang out from the lip on the near side, flowing across the narrow gap like a landslide that had lost its way and accidentally slid sideways instead of down.

"I heard rumors the Fast Rollers had a mission."

"Those are supposed to be secret," Tomas said.

Cameron shrugged. "People think being ugly means I'm deaf too. It's amazing how much I learn by pretending they're right."

Tomas frowned at the quickly growing bridge and growled, "Should be us with them."

Even Tomas could be right sometimes. "We have to get our second chance."

"Still no good way across," Tomas pointed out.

"Maybe," Cameron said, his eyes glued to the earthen bridge that had extended all the way across to the far side. More earth flowed across it, forming buttressed supports. In seconds, a sturdy bridge spanned the chasm, complete with a hard-packed surface to make marching easier.

Captain Hector spoke, and his voice carried easily to where Cameron and Tomas crouched in the darkness. "Into the pedra's lair, lads. You know your orders. We have five hours to complete our missions."

He marched onto the bridge, followed by the armored ranks of two dozen Fast Rollers Sergeant Rory hung back for a few seconds, then he and Garvin the Firetongue led the ten new recruits after.

As the troops marched over the gently arcing span, they tossed their torches aside, and the falling flames illuminated the impassable cliffs plunging down several hundred feet to the churning waters of the river far below. Masked by darkness, the black-armored soldiers seemed to melt into the night. The wind and the sounds of the distant river easily masked their footsteps.

Gregor was probably shielding their steps too. Like wraiths, they disappeared into the Grandurian mountains.

"That bridge," Tomas said, voicing Cameron's own thoughts.

"It's the best way," Cameron agreed. "But we step one foot on that thing and Gregor will know. He could seize us until they return, or just throw us into the chasm."

Tomas nodded, his brow furrowed as he considered the challenge. Neither of them possessed a tertiary elemental affinity, but they knew enough about how the tertiaries worked to understand the danger. While walking with earth, Gregor would sense any movement not shielded by solid stone, particularly across a construct that he created.

"Only one thing to do," Cameron decided, pointing toward the pile of rocks partway up the slope where the Fast Rollers had just descended. "We need an avalanche."

CHAPTER TEN

DANGER, MEN THINKING

Tomas gauged the distance from their safe perch to the rock pile clinging to the steep slope. It did look ready to fall, but they'd have to cover a lot of open ground.

"I don't think we can make it without Gregor sensing us."

"Maybe," Cameron said, his heavy brows furrowed in thought. "That chasm will make it harder on him to feel much on this side, I reckon."

"It would if he hadn't built an earth bridge across," Tomas said.

"Maybe he's not focused on anything this side of the bridge."

"And maybe your blind girlfriend will give you a passionate kiss when you see her again."

"I doubt it."

"Exactly."

Cameron blew out a frustrated breath. "There has to be a way. We need to get that torc, and that bridge is our best way across."

"Careful," Tomas cautioned. "You keep making arguments that well thought out and you'll pull a muscle in your brain."

"I'll risk it," Cameron said, although he started rubbing at his temple. "We need that avalanche to cover our run at the bridge."

Tomas considered the problem, and his head started to ache too. "If the chain was a bit longer, I could throw you, then you could pull me after."

"If the chain was longer, we wouldn't need the bridge."

Tomas couldn't help tapping some granite. It was his default reaction to any challenge. He adjusted the long rope on his shoulder, then blinked in surprise at as an idea blossomed in his mind like an unexpected sunrise.

"How about if we tie the chain and the rope together?" He glanced back toward the small meadow. "Over there the cliff's close enough that maybe we could throw each other across."

Cameron looked impressed. "Would be better than trying to outsmart Gregor on that bridge." He turned back to the bridge and frowned. "Although it would be a lot easier to just walk across."

"You'd never make it."

"I'd like to make sure, though." Cameron lifted a heavy rock and his armor creaked as he tapped deeply from his granite curse, then threw the rock. It smashed like a thunderclap into the base of the pile of rocks stuck on the slope. The sound echoed back and forth across the chasm and chunks of rock erupted from the impact point. With a groaning rumble that quickly built into a roaring cascade, the rock pile collapsed, releasing stones that eagerly tumbled down the slope, creating a respectable avalanche.

"Good throw," Tomas said. Cameron must have consumed half a day's portion with that effort. It would have consumed almost everything Tomas had left. He hoped Cameron was careful with whatever remained. They still had to track down and capture that torc.

As the avalanched roared down toward the bridge, the ground at the lip of the chasm reared up to catch the debris.

Tomas shook his head in silent wonder. "Tallan take Gregor. How can he shield the entire company and still have enough focus to play with this bridge?"

The avalanche slammed into the earthen barrier, shaking it, but not breaking through.

Cameron sighed. "That's their path of retreat."

"Are you satisfied that we can't get across that without Gregor sensing us?" Tomas asked.

"Not without thinking a lot harder," Cameron conceded.

"Better not risk it with another option handy," Tomas cautioned.

Throwing that rock to start the avalanche and prove whether or not Gregor was really paying attention was a good idea, and he worried Cameron might strain his mind if he tried out-thinking Gregor. He might not suffer the effects for a few minutes, and they couldn't afford to have him collapse when they needed to focus on slinging themselves across the chasm.

Together they returned to the edge of the chasm at the point where they'd lost the torc, careful to move across solid rock. Gregor was probably not paying attention to anything beyond the bridge on the Obrioner side, but it didn't pay to take chances.

"I think the chain and the rope together will be long enough," Cameron said after studying the gap for a moment.

Tomas uncoiled his rope and considered it with a critical eye. It was heavy line, so it would hold their weight, but was it long enough? Cameron had a little less than ten yards of chain, and the rope was just a bit longer. It would be close, but should be enough.

"Don't waste too much tying it," he cautioned as Cameron wove the end of the rope through several links of chain and tied it securely.

"If I use any less, they'll separate and you'll end up swimming home."

"You're talking like you assume I'll throw you across first."

Cameron rose to face him. "Of course."

He looked ready to fight over the point. As much as Tomas would love to punch that ugly face a few times to settle their nerves before they attempted the risky maneuver, he couldn't risk the powder.

"Fine."

Cameron blinked, unable to hide his surprise, and Tomas regretted the fact that he lacked enough powder to punch his partner as hard as he wanted to be hit. He'd have to pummel him that much harder during their next practice session.

He handed Cameron the end of the rope, stepped on the end of the chain with one foot, and pushed the lengths of rope and chain over the edge. Secured at both ends, they fell away into a long U-shape. He spotted no knots or kinks that might shorten the usable length.

"See you on the other side," Cameron grinned, and his leathers creaked as he tapped granite.

"Don't," Tomas reminded him. "Nothing but your legs until you're about to land."

"Right." Cameron blew out a breath, and for a second revealed a bit of nervousness. Tomas didn't blame him. He only had to cross about twenty yards, and with Tomas to help throw him, he should cover that distance easily. If for some reason he missed, and if Tomas dropped the chain or just decided to let go, he'd plummet all the way to the river hundreds of feet below.

He'd almost definitely survive the fall, but would he survive the river or find a way to climb back out? The hunt for the torc was becoming a very serious commitment.

Tomas didn't suggest Cameron back off, though. He couldn't afford to lose his second chance, and he needed Cameron to help him capture that torc, so he couldn't afford to let Cameron hesitate either.

So he clapped Cameron on the shoulder and said, "After you land, I'll signal when I'm ready to jump. Pull hard."

"Don't worry, partner. I'll get you across," Cameron assured him.

Tomas gripped a couple of Cameron's leather straps and tapped granite deeply. His reserves were already low enough that he faced a very real chance of running out before the night's adventure finished, but there was no other way. "On my mark."

Cameron nodded and crouched, ready to spring.
Tomas set himself and said, "Mark!"

He max-tapped granite and heaved just as Cameron launched himself into the air with all the force of his granite-enhanced legs. With the force of Tomas's throw added to his own jump, Cameron soared into the darkness like a stone flung from a catapult, with the rope trailing from one clenched fist.

Tomas grinned as he watched Cameron arc away toward the opposite side of the chasm. It was obvious they'd used more than enough strength to throw him those twenty yards to the far side. In fact, he looked like he'd hit the ground several yards beyond the edge.

The ramifications of that fact took a second too long to process with Tomas's muscles squeezing his brain the way they were. Their rope-chain was barely twenty yards long.

Even as he leaned down to snatch the end of the chain off the ground, Cameron soared over the edge of the Grandurian side of the chasm and tumbled into the clearing where the torc had landed moments before. The rope-chain reached went taught, and the end of the chain snapped out from under Tomas's foot.

As if in slow motion, he watched it falling away into the chasm, taking with it his only hope of reaching the far side, completing the torc hunt with Cameron, and winning his second chance.

Tomas jumped after it.

The movement was pure reflex, and only as he soared out over the deep, dark chasm like a flightless bird did he realize the insanity of what he'd just done.

Shouting a wordless cry that he hoped sounded more like a confident battle roar than a scream of terror, he focused his entire being on the dark lengths of chain falling through the deepening shadows like a pendulum. He couldn't help tapping granite again as he reached out with both hands, every muscle quivering with the need to catch that chain.

One finger brushed it, but failed to grab hold as his flight path angled more steeply downward, while the chain arced away toward the far side, pulled by the opposite, tethered end.

He made a final, desperate snatch for it, and his left hand closed around the very last links in the chain.

His plummeting fall turned into a graceful arc as the tip of the chain pulled him toward Granadure. He snatched at the chain with his other hand, but the movement only twisted him, and he missed. Even though he was max-tapping granite to his left hand, his hold was so tenuous, he feared the chain would slip free and release him to fall away into the depths.

He glanced down and stared into hundreds of feet of empty darkness stretching beneath his feet. He caught an impression more than a clear view of the churning river far below, and imagined the spraying foam, the treacherous currents, and the sharp rocks that he might shatter against if he fell.

Then he slammed into the vertical rock wall on the Grandurian side with a brutal impact that would have broken bones if not for the protection of his curse. He bounced off the rock face with a grunt of pain, and the chain slipped a fraction in his stone-hardened grip. He gasped, heart frozen with terror as he glanced up at the last two links of chain barely clutched between his fingers, all that connected him to his partner above.

With a convulsion of every muscle in his body, driven by max-tapped granite and terror, Tomas heaved upward, legs scrabbling against the rough stone of the cliff, and caught the chain with his right hand. With both hands now gripping it so hard that one of the links actually bent under the force, he was finally able to breathe again.

Then the chain rattled against the stones and rose a foot. Cameron must have found his feet and had begun hauling him up.

Tomas resisted the urge to call to him to hurry. He lacked the breath for it, and he feared his voice would sound high-pitched and scared. He glanced back across the chasm at the slightly higher Obrioner side, so close but so incredibly far away, and could scarce believe he'd leaped off that cliff after the chain.

He started to laugh, and the unfamiliar fear that had rattled him so deeply started to fade just a little.

Cameron grabbed his arm and yanked him onto the stone lip beside him. Tomas rolled farther from the edge and had to resist the urge to kiss the stone under foot.

"You're cracked and splintered," Cameron said, shaking his head, a look of grudging admiration on his face. "I can't believe you jumped."

"Someone has to do the hard work around here," Tomas said with a shrug. "Can't count on you for anything useful."

Cameron grunted, separated the chain from the rope, and started looping the chain over his shoulder again. "Well, you're crazy enough to be a Firetongue, that's a fact. Stop slacking off and congratulating yourself. Won't be fun beating you if you're just going to lie there all night."

Tomas grunted as he climbed back to his feet and forced himself to release his curse and preserve the last of his waning granite. "You're getting as blind as your girlfriend. You were supposed to land near the edge, not roll like a giant Tumble-Tosser ball across that meadow."

"Ungrateful stench vat," Cameron muttered as he moved up the slope of the meadow, following the signs of destruction left by the torc.

"Ugly illiterate," Tomas replied with a smile.

"You don't even know what that word means," Cameron said over his shoulder.

"Sure I do. It means you don't know how to use a fork and knife at the same time."

Cameron grunted. "Forks are evil distractions invented by women."

As the two followed the trail of snapped brush and gouged earth, Tomas was grateful the clouds had cleared. On this side of the chasm, the rising moon was blocked by the shadow of a high Grandurian peak. A little light would help, but Tomas didn't think Cameron had developed any secondary affinity. Although Tomas did have a confirmed secondary affinity with limestone, the stars shed far more light than the strongest glow he had ever produced.

"You know, I've been thinking," Tomas said after another minute.

Cameron grunted. "Sure that's wise? Footing is pretty treacherous here."

"I can manage if we don't go too fast. When we catch that torc, you realize I need it as much as you do."

"It's my torc," Cameron insisted.

"But Fast Rollers work in pairs. You can't get a second chance without me."

Cameron paused and turned to face him. "If you help me catch my torc and get it back to Merkland, I'll put in a good word for you with the captain."

Tomas chuckled. "More like you'll end up helping me, and I put in a good word for you."

Cameron thought about that, rubbing his temples with both hands. He had definitely strained that noggin with so much thinking in one night. "How about this? First one to subdue the torc gets to claim it, and the other agrees to act as assistant."

"Deal."

They clasped hands, and Tomas felt a thrill of anticipation. They might be about to scramble up a dark ravine in enemy territory with their granite strength nearly spent, but the contest was shaping up to be legendary.

Then Cameron tapped granite and threw Tomas over his shoulder.

Tomas cursed as he slid to the very lip of the chasm. The recent near-fall into the river so far below triggered a flash of fear that delayed him another couple seconds. By the time he regained his feet and turned back up the ravine, Cameron was bounding up the steep slope after the missing torc.

Tomas followed as fast as he could, but he didn't dare tap any granite. As he scrambled up the hill in darkness, crashing through tough scrub brush and banging his shins on hidden rocks, he started softly humming his favorite battle song.

CHAPTER ELEVEN

SOME KITTIES ARE NOT MEANT FOR PETTING

The Kinbrace outpost was manned.

Rory surveyed the tiny outpost from a rocky ledge on the flank of a mountain about a quarter of a mile to the southwest. The long Kinbrace valley ran below his position, leading up to the outpost which commanded a magnificent view of the area. The valley ran southwest for over two miles between rugged mountains, almost all the way to the border chasm. The mountain lording over the northeast corner of the valley, just behind the fort, was so steep, Rory doubted anyone could climb it.

The fort enjoyed a great location. Well, it would if either country had found a use for the beautiful but remote valley. So the outpost had never been expanded, and was usually empty.

Not anymore. Torches burned along the walls, declaring the little fort was occupied. The outer wall was little more than a square, wooden palisade, about fifty yards on each side. No interior structure showed above the palisade, and from Rory's briefing, he doubted any structure inside was more than a single story.

All in all, it was a pretty disappointing target for his first incursion across the border. Still, finding someone there was more interesting than finding nothing.

"I could incinerate that wall without even needing a deep burn," Garvin muttered for the fourth time since they had started observing the distant outpost.

"I thought you said you sensed a Flameweaver in there," Rory said.

Garvin shrugged. "That pile of sticks would burn so fast, I doubt he could stop it."

"Tempting," Rory admitted. "But our orders are clear. We are not to initiate hostilities."

He couldn't let Garvin know he shared the man's eagerness to attack and test his new company against the Grandurians. His little band might be made up of the newest Fast Rollers, but he would bet on his men against any Grandurian Rumblers.

The problem was, he didn't know what other powers the Grandurians could bring to bear. Garvin would eagerly duel the Flameweaver, but if any other tertiaries were stationed in that fort, it wouldn't matter how tough Rory's company might be. Bash fighters couldn't compete with Petralists who wielded the might of the elements. At best, they'd be sent scurrying back to Obrion. More likely they'd be captured.

He doubted the Grandurians would intentionally kill any of them. Skirmishes during a time of peace usually resulted in embarrassing negotiations for the losing side and huge payments of gold and power stones to secure the return of the captured soldiers.

"So we're just going to leave?" Garvin asked.

Several of the soldiers crouched nearby leaned closer to listen. In the darkness, Rory could only make out the closest of the group. Maknab was a talented soldier, but he had the tiniest ankles Rory had ever seen. He hoped the man never got into a max-tapped pushing match because those tiny ankles might just crack under the pressure.

"Not necessarily. My orders are also to gather intelligence."

Garvin rubbed his hands together, dripping a few crimson sparks.

"Watch the flames," Rory cautioned.

He couldn't afford to let Garvin get distracted. Walking with fire was notoriously hard on discipline. Immersing oneself in the flames tended to fry Firetongues' restraint, and if Garvin wasn't careful, he could easily slip into a marble-induced frenzy and blow their cover. Of course, then Rory would have to let his Fast Rollers fight.

Tempting, if he knew which Petralists they faced.

Garvin concealed the flames and said, "So I burn down the palisade and spank their Flameweaver while you boys bash the regulars and get whatever intelligence you need."

Rory sighed. If only life could be so simple. "You're forgetting that we're Fast Rollers. We're supposed to be good at getting intelligence without starting a war."

"Waste of time," Garvin muttered.

"Perhaps, but we have to try."

"What if they've got a Sapper or Water Moccasin?"

Rory considered that. "I doubt they have a Water Moccasin. Not enough water in this area to justify one. But a Sapper is the question, isn't it?"

"How do you propose to find out?"

"I propose you find out."

"I thought you didn't want me burning down the place," Garvin said, his eyes starting to glow as muted little flames began dancing across the back of his orbs. It was an unnerving sight, and Rory wondered if Garvin even felt the pain any more.

"I don't. I want you to summon something and send it up there to scout around."

"Good idea," Garvin admitted. "But no guarantee the Sapper will take the bait."

"If the ground doesn't swallow it on the reconnaissance run, have it start digging under the back wall. If that doesn't raise an alarm, then there's no Sapper worth the name inside."

"I like it," Garvin chuckled, exposing teeth lined with little white flames.

Garvin possessed a primary affinity with granite, a necessary ingredient for summoning, since all summoned creatures were formed with one of the elements, wrapped in a granite shell. Garvin led the way back around the flank of the knoll. There he could work while the hillside obscured the glow of his fire from any watchers or Longseers who might be stationed on the Kinbrace wall. He crouched near the ground and shoved his hand in a spare pouch of granite powder to absorb another hefty portion.

"The Flameweaver won't sense the summoning?" Rory asked, suddenly wondering if the idea was as clever as he had thought.

Garvin's eyes lit with dancing flames and he shook his head, scattering tiny burning droplets from his eyes. "I doubt he's actively tapping marble anyway, but even if he is, he'd have to be working flames pretty far out to feel the heat of what I'm doing. Summoning is all directed inward, so there's almost nothing for him to feel."

"Good. Make it quick."

Garvin chuckled. "You think working a deep burn is easy, sergeant?"

"Not at all," Rory said in a calm tone to help Garvin avoid slipping into a marble insanity that would guarantee something rash to wreck the plan. "But if you couldn't do it, you wouldn't be here, would you?"

"Point," Garvin said, and a little glowing one appeared in the air above his left shoulder.

The Firetongue fell silent as he hunkered over his work. His posture became rigid as he focused the wild flames burning through him into a granite-shelled image he needed to hold fixed in his mind. Rory rarely wished for anything more than a bash fight, but he had to admit he would enjoy the ability to summon creatures at will to assist in his work.

Light began to glow above the ground in front of Garvin, forming an intense, tiny rainbow that bent back upon itself. As Fast Rollers shifted closer to help shield the light, the summoning abruptly concluded with a muted thunderclap.

A half-sized nuall hunting cat appeared on the ground in front of Garvin, already crouched to spring, the tip of its black tail lashing side to side. Its eyes glowed with crimson flames, the only indication of which element had given it life.

Garvin petted the creature, which was about as big as a medium-sized dog, and its eyes faded to soft amber. It was a pretty impressive summoning. He must have consumed half a piece of marble to produce enough concentrated fire to create it.

Rory said, "Good work. Let's see if it can make it to the fort. Men, be prepared to move out if a Sapper responds."

The hunting cat leaped almost before Rory finished speaking. It shot between Rory's legs in a flash and disappeared around the knoll, racing for the valley and the outpost fort on the upper end. By the time Rory returned to the position to see the torches of the distant fort, the nuall was lost to the darkness.

"Where is it?" one of the Fast Rollers asked.

Garvin had followed more slowly, a far-off look on his face. The nuall was not independently conscious, and part of his mind and attention ran with the little cat through the darkness. That distraction was one of the greatest dangers to tertiary Petralists during a summoning, but with the Fast Rollers around to protect him in case of a surprise attack, Garvin could focus more attention on the scouting mission without fear.

Garvin raised a hand and pointed. "We're halfway across the valley already. The earth has not attacked yet."

"If there's a Sapper, he'll feel the cat coming, and no doubt it'll seem odd that a hunting cat will close so fast on the outpost."

"Do you want me to take a more roundabout route?" Garvin asked.

"No. The most important need is to unearth any Sapper."

"No pun intended?" Garvin smiled.

The next two minutes dragged. Rory was pleased to note that his men seemed comfortable waiting and made no unnecessary movements or talking. Many bash fighters hated forced immobility, but his new squad was performing exactly as well as he had hoped.

"I've circled the outpost twice," Garvin reported eventually. "And I'm digging beneath the back wall now."

Rory breathed a little easier. If a Sapper had destroyed the summoned nuall, the enemy would have been alerted to the presence of enemy forces, and they would have been forced to retreat. For a moment he considered the fact that maybe he should have requested a flying summoning first. Garvin could have reconnoitered the outpost silent and unseen from above and perhaps spotted a Sapper, who would probably be stationed on a telltale tower of earth. He decided not to mention the mistake, but file it away for future use, if a similar situation presented itself.

"Make it big enough so I can fit," he said instead.

"You're taking us in?" Macnab asked eagerly.

"No. You will all remain at the reinforcement alert distance of one hundred yards. Should I run into trouble, you will attack with full prejudice."

Garvin rubbed his hands. "I don't usually wish you trouble, Sergeant, but tonight I'm thinking it would be fun."

"Fun will have to wait. We've got work to do," Rory said. As much as he longed to leap into a bash fight with the Grandurians, returning to Captain Hector with important intelligence would be far more satisfying.

"Do you think it's wise for you to enter that fort alone?" Macnab dared ask.

"The more people we try to smuggle in there, the more likely we'll get discovered," Rory said. "With Garvin's nuall helping to scout ahead, I should be able to infiltrate easily enough and see if I can learn anything about this Grandurian company, who their commander is, and what they're dong here."

Macnab said, "With all due respect, sir, shouldn't one of us do that? We're supposed to shield our leaders from harm."

That was a valid point, although Rory was a lead from the front sort of officer, and he hated the idea of sending other men into danger that perhaps he could handle better. "I appreciate the offer, but you haven't completed your training. I'm the best qualified for this insertion." He clapped Macnab on the shoulder and added, "Study hard, and maybe next time you'll be ready to go in instead."

Macnab shared an eager grin with his partner. Rory didn't doubt they'd be ready next time. He'd have to prepare a better justification to take the risk himself anyway.

"I'm through," Garvin reported. "Came up behind the water barrels. It's a well shielded spot."

"Good." Rory allowed a smile, the only sign of his growing excitement. He had wanted a chance to close with Grandurians on a mission like this ever since Hector had chosen him to help build the Fast Rollers.

He strode toward the valley floor, not bothering to sneak yet. With no Sappers or Longseers watching the valley, he'd easily blend into the night until he drew closer to the fort.

"I'm going in."

CHAPTER TWELVE

PARTNERS GO DOWN TOGETHER

ameron grinned as he reached the top of the steep, narrow ravine he had followed for a quarter mile. Cameron wasn't much of a tracker, but angry torcs were easy to follow. He was panting from the fast climb, but the exertion was a small price to pay. He glanced back down into the deeper shadows of the ravine, but couldn't see Tomas.

He could hear him, though. If Cameron was careful, he should have enough powder left to capture the torc and get it back as far as the bridge. Tomas must be running even lower on powder because he hadn't tapped any to help with the climb, and he had lagged steadily farther behind.

"Lack of preparation on your part means it hurts more when I clobber you," Cameron muttered, then turned to scan the open slope he had reached.

The moon was still blocked by the higher peaks, but now that he was out of the confines of the deep ravine, the landscape seemed far brighter under the brilliant blanket of stars. The night was turning colder, and Cameron breathed deep, enjoying the thought of stealing Grandurian air.

The ravine had led up to a saddle between two moderate peaks that rose to the east and west. A trail of trampled bushes and trees slashed by the torc's tusks ran straight up that saddle to the north. Smaller saplings had been sheared off completely.

Cameron was happy that the torc hadn't suffered major damage by that tumble across the chasm. He didn't want to deliver a broken torc to Captain Hector, but a mighty beast that had fought valiantly until he vanquished it.

As he trotted up the slope, Cameron wondered what the Fast Rollers were doing in Granadure. Tensions were always high along the border, despite the long peace that other parts of the nation claimed to be enjoying. He doubted the company were planning a substantial raid that might spark a war, but then why risk the incursion?

Cameron thumped himself on the side of the head to break out of the useless thinking. He must be more tired than he thought. He was usually wise enough to leave thinking to the officers.

Twenty minutes later, he reached the summit of the saddle and stifled a groan. The mountains continued to rise on either side, forming a high canyon that he was still climbing through. He'd only managed to summit the first long rise. The canyon ahead was a little more lush than the ravine he'd recently left behind. The ground changed from solid rock to long mountain grasses, and dark clumps of shadows suggested bushes and trees scattered widely across the open slope that continued to rise toward yet another ridge.

He paused to listen, but heard no sound of the torc. He did hear distant cursing from Tomas, but his partner must have fallen even farther behind because the sound was barely a whisper, a vague promise that Tomas indeed planned to make the hunt a challenge.

Cameron started forward again. He didn't want to remain in Granadure all night. Captain Hector had said the Fast Rollers had about five hours to complete their mission, and Cameron planned to be waiting at the bridge with the bound torc in hand to greet them.

Smiling at the thought, he broke into a jog up the valley. The torc had stopped wrecking the landscape, but there was only one direction it could have gone. Black gouges in the soil might be tracks, but Cameron wouldn't know a torc track unless the beast stomped on Tomas's face. He lacked the light to inspect the marks anyway.

Half an hour later, he reached the top end of the long canyon and scanned the new vista. The mountain to his left fell away into lower hills that bordered a long valley that ran a couple miles toward the southwest. The mountain to the right, which should be east, rose higher and joined an even higher peak to the north, which rose in steep cliffs, blocking the way straight ahead.

The ridge where he stood continued to run north, rising toward that steep cliff. The land to the left fell away sharply, while the slope to the right changed to craggy rocks that would make an attempted ascent that way nearly impossible. The ridge he was following narrowed as it climbed northward. Deep shadows made it impossible to tell if it dead-ended against that cliff, or if there was another path from there.

Cameron paused to study the slope dropping down toward the distant valley to his left. The torc probably continued up the ridge, but if it turned left at the point where Cameron stood, it could have angled down toward that other valley. As he scanned that lower, shadowed landscape, he was surprised to notice lights. After a moment's study he realized what he was looking at. A small, square fort was positioned near the base of the steep northern mountain, right at the top end of that valley. It was clearly manned. The distance was too great for Cameron to see specifics, but just knowing that he had found a Grandurian outpost lent more urgency to his hunt.

"By the Tallan's wretched memory, where'd you get to?" Cameron muttered.

He paced up the rocky ground of the ridge, scanning for any sign the torc might have passed, wishing he had a huntsman along to help him find the cursed beast. A moment later, he heard the distant huffing grunt of the torc and grinned.

It hadn't turned left into that long valley, but had continued up the ridge. Cameron trotted in that direction and pulled the heavy chains from his shoulder. "You got yourself cornered, you have."

He followed the ridge another quarter mile as it continued to rise above the little valley. As he approached the cliffs of the northern peak, the slope to his left fell away at an even steeper angle. He doubted the torc would risk attempting to descend that. As long as no canyon opened in the hillside to his right, the torc was trapped.

Cameron slowed to a cautious walk, chain at shoulder height, ready to throw, squinting into the darkness.

There! Movement in the darkness, like an enormous shadow farther up the ridge. It was only about fifty yards ahead of him, moving away, nearly lost in the darkness.

Cameron gave chase, breaking into a run, savoring the feeling of impending battle and tapping his curse. The ridge was barely twenty feet wide. The torc couldn't slip past him without giving him a chance to tackle it, but he had enough room to maneuver if it charged him. He applied granite to his entire body, ready to close with the torc, but held it at the minimum tap rate to preserve the powder until the moment of action.

The cliff to the north reared high into the night, barely a hundred yards away. When he glanced over the drop-off to his left and scanned the long valley, he was tempted to stop and find a big rock to push over the edge. If it tumbled all the way down, it would reach the valley floor about three hundred yards below his position, right near that little fort. If it got the right kind of roll, it could smash into the palisade wall.

Tempting, but he didn't have spare powder for games like that. Besides, he couldn't afford to alert the Grandurians that he was up there, or they might interrupt his torc hunt. It was infuriating that he had to choose between capturing his second chance and striking at the enemies he'd trained for years to defeat.

Finally he spotted the torc. The beast had reached the cliff blocking the way to the north and was pacing back toward Cameron, not far from the drop-off. Cameron grinned. There was no other exit after all. A shadow along the face of the northern cliff might be a narrow trail, but it was far too narrow for the torc's bulky shoulders.

"Now be a good beastie and give me a real fight here at the end," Cameron urged as he closed to within fifty feet of the huge animal.

It looked tired. The horn in the center of its heavy head was bent, and one of the tusks looked cracked. It swayed where it stood, but it grunted in reply and pawed the ground with those sharply cloven hooves.

"That's right," Cameron urged. "You won't go down without a fight." This torc had given them enough trouble that he hoped for a final confrontation. He didn't have the powder for a long fight with the beast, but he didn't need much time. He knew what to expect now, and he would have his second chance.

The torc huffed again, a deep growling grunt that escalated into a snorting call. Cameron threw out his hands and shouted, "Come on!"

The torc trumpeted that same angry sound it had the first time they met, and it charged. Cameron ran to meet it, tapping more granite and laughing with the thrill of a good hunt finally reaching its end.

As the torc charged in its odd galloping gait, Cameron threw the heavy chain, looping it over the beast's head, then jumped into the air.

The torc tried to impale him with its horn, but it forgot the lance was bent and missed by an inch. Cameron tried to snatch its head, but he'd jumped too high and missed by half a foot. It thew its head up as it galloped beneath him, catching his thighs with its wide, armored forehead, flipping him feet-high into the air. He laughed with the thrill of fighting such a massive beast, and threw a second length of chain even as he landed face-first on its wide shoulders and tumbled along the creature's long back.

The chains caught the torc in the foreleg and tripped it. It crashed to the ground and rolled. Cameron landed nearby and regained his feet first. As the beast struggled to rise, he leaped upon it, jumping right between the deadly, thrashing hooves and wrapping length after length of chain around them. That close, the beast's heavy breathing was like a bellows in his ears, and its thick, musky scent clung to Cameron's face and throat. Its hide was hard, like leathery stone.

It tried to heave itself back to its feet, but Cameron punched it in the ribs and knocked it back over again. In seconds, he secured the monster and stood over it, lifting his hands in victory and shouting a wordless cry of joy.

He didn't see the tree trunk until Tomas used it to club him in the ribs. The blow knocked him flying along the edge of the ridge, cursing himself for a fool. How could he fall for Tomas's sneak attack twice in one night? It was disgustingly incompetent. As he skidded thirty feet, leaving deep scars on the rocky ground, his anger grew with every bounce and scrape.

"Thanks for chaining up my torc," Tomas laughed, leaning on his ten-foot club, one foot resting on the angry torc's flank. It lay at the edge of the ridge, right over the steep drop-off toward the valley below. Cameron hadn't realized how close he'd come to losing the monster over the edge while struggling to chain it. "You really need to pay more attention to your surroundings. Haven't you paid attention to anything we've been learning recently?" The beast trumpeted in anger and thrashed within the chains, but could not break free.

"My torc," Cameron snapped as he stalked closer, fists clenched, ready to beat Tomas all the way back to the border chasm and let him fall in this time. He restrained the urge to max-tap granite. He'd used too much in the frantic effort to secure the torc and might not even have enough to drag the huge beast back to the border. He needed Tomas's help, but he needed to put his partner in his place first. "I did all the work to capture it."

"And I'm taking all the credit, just like officers should."

"You're no officer," Cameron growled. There were no other trees nearby, so he couldn't get his own club, but he didn't need one anyway. He charged.

Tomas lunged to meet him, swinging the club hard enough that the blow would probably send Cameron soaring back to Obrion if it hit.

Cameron dropped under the blow, sliding across the ground and kicking Tomas's feet out from under him. Tomas fell onto him and Cameron punched him in the face in greeting.

The two rolled over each other, pummeling one another in unrestrained bash-fighting fury as they rolled down the slope of the ridge away from the chained torc. Cameron only let himself enjoy the the contest for a few seconds, though. He just didn't have the powder for it. Tomas surely had even less powder than he did, and it was he who broke away first.

Rolling away from Cameron's latest punch, he kicked out with both feet, catching Cameron in the chest. He slid twenty feet back up the ridge and slammed to a stop against something solid.

His torc. The impact rolled it half over, and it trumpeted angrily and convulsed within the restraining loops of chain. One rear leg slipped over the edge, followed by the other. With a final twist, the beast rolled off the ridge and onto the slope. It continued to heave and twist within the chains, the wild movements setting it spinning faster and faster down the slope toward the distant valley.

"You Tallan-blasted idiot," Cameron exclaimed as he jumped to his feet. "We don't have enough powder left to carry that thing all the way back up here." He'd done it, had chased his second chance all the way into Granadure, run it to ground, and chained it.

Now it was gone, and he had no idea how they were going to get it back.

Tomas joined him at the edge, staring down the slope at the still-rolling torc that looked like it planned to tumble all the way down to the valley floor. He blew out a breath and rounded on Cameron.

"All you had to do was admit I won it, and we could be carrying it back down already."

"I chained it! We could have won our second chance together, idiot. Now what are we going to do?"

Tomas glared and threw a punch.

Cameron ducked under it, grabbed Tomas in a bear hug, and squeezed. Tomas would run out of powder first, and he'd squeeze the man until his ribs cracked.

Tomas apparently realized the danger too, and he lunged back and forth, trying to break Cameron's hold while beating uselessly on his stone-hardened head.

They shifted along the edge of the ridge, straining mightily against each other. Tomas fought hard, punching and kneeing and twisting, but Cameron held on tight. He was sick and tired of Tomas interrupting his hunt. The man seemed intent on learning the hard way how they handled idiots like that here in the north country, and Cameron was happy to oblige.

Then Tomas heaved against him and he stepped back, but found nothing but air. For a second the two of them teetered, on the verge of following the torc down the steep slope.

"Let go," Tomas growled.

"And fall without you? Not a chance." Time to teach. "Hold on, partner."

He pulled, and together they toppled backward off the ridge and down the slope.

CHAPTER THIRTEEN

LOOK, BUT DON'T TOUCH

ory crawled into the Kinbrace outpost, feeling relieved as he pulled himself out of the narrow hole that Garvin's nuall had dug under the wall. The hole hadn't been quite wide enough, so Rory had been forced to release granite entirely to shrink to his smallest size and claw through without the aid of his curse. He'd gotten stuck halfway through and the little nuall had grabbed one of his shoulder straps in its teeth and hauled him the rest of the way in a shower of dirt.

Now he crouched in the darkness, just inside the back wall of the fort, behind a row of tall water barrels. As he brushed dirt from his hair and face, he considered the black-coated, summoned nuall sitting in front of him. If not for the softly glowing amber eyes, he never would have seen it, even sitting that close.

"I didn't realized summoned creatures were so strong," Rory whispered.

The nuall grinned in reply, exactly like Garvin would, its teeth momentarily outlined with fire.

The fort smelled of wood smoke and fresh-cut lumber. The scents were all mixed with the constant smell of earth that clung to Rory. He rose to a crouch and peered around the enemy camp.

The inside of the fort was even less inspiring than the outside. The palisade wall encircling the fort was manned by only three sentries on each side, but none of them were Longseers. Any Longseer would have heard the nuall digging, or would have certainly heard Rory's grunting and panting as he struggled to crawl under the wall. By their uniforms, the sentries looked like regulars, and sleepy ones at that.

Inside the walls, there were actually no buildings at all. The large command tent dominated the northern end of the fort, positioned not far from where he crouched. It looked like maybe one lantern was lit inside, and a pair of soldiers stood guard at the entryway.

The center of the fort was only about twenty-five yards away, and the only permanent structure stood there. Clearly raised by a Sapper at some point in the past, the earthen cooking area was hardened to brick. A wide fireplace sported several cooking arms and racks, while four separate ovens were stacked in pairs to either side. The brick construct flowed into long tables that extended out like arms and would make excellent work areas for preparing meals. On the end of the left-side table, the earth had been formed into a smooth-sided cistern of water, probably filled by the water barrels Rory was using for cover.

The rest of the camp was tidy and ordered, as he would expect from a military company. Three long rows of two-man tents were arranged beneath the western palisade wall to his right. Rory counted thirty in all. Few soldiers were in sight, so most of those tents would be occupied by sleeping men. Of the five soldiers visible at ground level, three wore the uniform of Grandurian regulars, while the other two wore the shifting battle leathers of Rumblers.

Rory wasn't sure which nation had first developed the expandable battle armor for their bash fighters, but the design made so much sense, he wasn't surprised that both countries used virtually the same approach.

He wished he could tell how much of the force was made up of unenhanced regulars, and how many Rumblers. There was no way to know unless he poked his head in every tent. That wasn't why he had come.

Moving slowly in the darkness, Rory crept from behind the water barrels, keeping close to the rough planks of the northern wall. The packed earth underfoot made it easy to walk quietly as he moved to the rear of the command tent. Every command tent he had ever seen was set up the same way inside. The bulk of the tent would be open, centered around a command table. Space at the back would be reserved for the commander and perhaps a handful of aids or other officers to bunk. No guards had been posted at the rear of the tent, so Rory continued circling to the far side.

He stopped when the outer curve of the round tent still blocked him from view of anyone loitering near the fire, positioning himself as close to where he presumed the command table stood as possible. He didn't want to slip into the tent and trip over the sleeping commander.

Drawing a razor sharp little knife, Rory carefully sliced a tiny hole in the canvas. The blade parted the heavy fabric easily and made no sound as he slowly drew it down just far enough to make a hole he could peek through.

Placing his eye to the hole, Rory looked. He hoped to see the single lantern illuminating sleeping officers who would not notice him slip past to steal their papers.

Instead he saw General Wolfram standing barely three feet away.

The sight gave Rory a jolt of half dread and half excitement. He had never seen Wolfram in person, but the man standing at the command table, turned three quarters away from Rory, could be no other man. He was tall, with broad shoulders and salt-and-pepper hair, but his distinguishing feature was the excellent handlebar mustache.

With a single slash of his dagger, Rory could rip through the tent and lunge inside to do battle with the clever commander who Chornail Carbrey had dubbed the Old Wolf.

As eager as he was to prove himself against the man who was renowned as particularly deadly, even among the Blades, he restrained himself. The mission was not to engage Wolfram and rouse the entire camp. Even if he managed to defeat the deadly officer, the ruckus would draw in the rest of his company for a full attack. They would level the fort and either capture or kill everyone inside. Beyond the risk to his tiny company facing those odds, such an attack might trigger war.

His mission was not to start a war. So Rory waited, barely daring to breathe as he peered into the tent. The table where Wolfram worked was covered with the expected assortment of scrolls and maps, but Rory would need a moment or two of undisturbed time to scan them and find the intelligence he was seeking.

Somewhere on that table, if Hector's spy was correct, Rory would find a map and information detailing a new, secret quarry somewhere in the mountains nearby. Rory was prepared to remain standing there outside the tent all night if that's what it took to get that intelligence.

Unfortunately, waiting that long might lead to other problems. Wolfram did not look like he planned to move any time soon. Rory needed a distraction.

He considered calling upon Garvin's summoned nuall again, but every idea he came up with led to pitched battle.

For the first time in a very long time, Rory was not sure what to do.

CHAPTER FOURTEEN

Everyone Understands Family Problems

he world spun as Tomas bounced down the steep slope with Cameron still holding on like a leech. At least the battering they were taking had forced Cameron to ease his hold a bit. Tomas managed to reduce his tap rate between crushing impacts, daring the risk of misjudging one and suffering broken bones in order to preserve his fast-waning granite powder. He'd never imagined running out of powder when he really needed it. If not for Alban's tap-rate management lessons, he would have already run out.

The only good thing about Cameron holding on like that was that he hit the ground first about half the time, sparing Tomas some of the brutal impacts. The slope wasn't exactly vertical, but it was steep enough that there was no way they could hope to slow or stop their wild tumble until they reached the valley far below.

They spun faster and faster as they fell, until Tomas loss all sense of direction. He squeezed his eyes shut and clamped his mouth closed to try holding in his dinner as his stomach made more and more energetic flipping sensations in his gut.

He wasn't even sure when they reached the valley, but all of a sudden he realized they were tumbling sideways more than down, and the impacts weren't quite so brutal. He opened his eyes just in time to see a set of wide, wooden gates in a palisade wall just before the two of them exploded right through the gates like stone shot from a catapult.

The final impact broke Cameron's hold and the two of them tumbled side by side for another eighty feet before crashing into a brick oven that rose out of the smooth earthen ground in the middle of the fort.

Bricks and still-burning embers exploded away in every direction, knocking down several small tents and setting two more on fire. As Tomas staggered to his feet, then nearly fell over because his head had decided to keep spinning, he dimly became aware of voices raised in alarm.

After another second, he realized he didn't understand what they were saying. They were speaking Grandurian. Tomas punched himself in the side of the head to get his thoughts to settle down, then really looked around.

They had tumbled down the slope and plowed right into the Grandurian fort. Cameron was just coming to his feet next to Tomas, looking as disoriented as Tomas felt. So Tomas punched him in the side of the head to help him recover.

Cameron collapsed, but bounded back to his feet a second later. In that second, Tomas noted the rows of orderly tents with scores of soldiers erupting out of them. The regulars were easy to spot. They were the men who weren't swelling with impossibly huge muscles, but who looked uncomfortable, dressed only in smallclothes. There were a few Rumblers mixed in with them, but he spotted fewer than ten.

A full Grandurian company, and he and Cameron had fallen right into the middle of it.

He turned to share the good news with Cameron just in time for his partner to shove a fist halfway down Tomas's throat. The blow knocked him off his feet, giving Cameron a chance to look around and realize where they were.

Tomas jumped back to his feet and faced Cameron. He wanted nothing more than to leap into battle against the Grandurians, but he was almost out of powder, and a bash fight like that would consume far more than he had available.

Cameron seemed to realize the danger at the same time and gestured Tomas closer. "Hit me."

Tomas wasn't sure how that was going to help, but he was willing to try. So he punched Cameron again. He didn't max-tap granite, but only tapped enough to keep from breaking his fingers.

Cameron rocked back from the blow anyway and threw a punch at Tomas in turn. The two of them had sparred together long enough that Tomas recognized that Cameron was also holding back, allowing him to shepherd his own fading reserves, but still look like they were bashing enthusiastically.

As the Grandurians drew into an unbroken circle around the two of them, Tomas and Cameron continued pounding on each other.

Cameron shouted, "You will not dishonor her again, pedra-dung-licking-cabbage-sniffer!"

It took Tomas a few seconds and three more hits to the head before he realized what Cameron was playing at. In a recent briefing about Granadure, they'd learned about an odd aspect to the nation's honor code, specific to Rumblers. Brothers were honor bound to challenge any potential suitors to single combat to prove they were worthy. It seemed far too reasonable a custom to be Grandurian, but they might be able to leverage it until they figured out what to do.

A Grandurian Rumbler stepped out of the encircling soldiers. This man was actually dressed in battle leathers and he held up his hands for the two of them to stop fighting for a moment.

"What are having do here?" he asked in such broken Obrioner that Tomas barely understood.

"We're fighting, of course," Tomas said.

The Rumbler frowned in concentration and Cameron added, "Honor battle."

The man's expression lifted and he said, "Ah. Fight honor sister?"

"Uh, yeah," Tomas said, looking to see if Cameron had any idea what that meant."

"Sure," Cameron said with a grin. He pointed at Tomas and shouted, "His sister."

The Rumbler said something in Grandurian and the other soldiers stopped scowling and instead smiled and motioned the two of them to fight on.

Tomas jumped at Cameron and closed in a grappling hold. He was amazed when several of the Grandurians cheered. "Can you believe this is working?"

"They're crazy," Cameron whispered back as they struggled together, making it look like they were max-tapping their strength.

"I know. Can't they see how ugly you are? No sister of mine would fall for you."

Cameron's expression turned thoughtful. "Maybe Grandurian women don't care so much about how you look."

If anything might ever tempt Cameron to defect over the border, the promise of a woman might just do it.

Tomas couldn't risk letting him dwell on that possibility, so he punched Cameron in the nose hard enough to shake loose the distracting thoughts. "Focus, partner. If we give them a good show, maybe they'll share some granite so we can keep going."

Cameron grinned. "Then we bash them all down."

He hoped the Grandurians were that dumb because he was almost out of granite. Still, bash fighting was easier than thinking, so he threw himself into the duel with enthusiasm. He and Cameron bashed across the fort, carefully managing their tap rates to minimize the burn while trying to give the Grandurians the best show possible.

Tomas hoped they could fight right out through the gate, but the same soldier who had spoken with them earlier, pushed them the other way and said, "Fight middle. Many light."

Tomas was tempted to punch the man, but that might start the very brawl he couldn't afford to begin. So he punched Cameron again and reluctantly moved back toward the center of camp.

As they fought, the soldiers cheered them on with growing enthusiasm. Most of them hadn't bothered to get dressed, and Tomas appreciated the fact that they had their priorities straight. He wasn't sure how they decided which of the two to cheer for, but as long as they were cheering, they wouldn't be beating the two of them to a pulp.

124

Then the cheering abruptly stopped.

The ring of Grandurian soldiers parted, and a tall man strode through. He wore only a single sword on his belt, but he moved with the unmistakable grace of an Allcarver. The long, handlebar mustache he wore marked him better than even his officer uniform.

General Wolfram.

CHAPTER FIFTEEN

WHO KNEW IDIOTS COULD BE SO HELPFUL?

ory tensed when the cries of alarm began.

Had Garvin decided to get creative when he realized Rory was stuck, with no way to proceed? Or had he also recognized Wolfram and thought to create an excuse for Rory to attack, despite his orders?

He tapped granite, applying it to his entire body in preparation for ripping apart the canvas and attacking. If his men were indeed discovered, he would need to remove Wolfram quickly. The resulting confusion might provide the vital bit of advantage they would need to survive.

A half-dressed soldier rushed into the tent as Wolfram began striding around the table to investigate the commotion.

Wolfram spoke in Grandurian, his voice calm despite the unexpected alarm in the dead of night. Rory assumed he was asking what was going on.

The soldier responded, and Wolfram looked surprised. Rory wished he understood Grandurian. He needed to know.

The nuall clawed at his leg. Rory crouched beside it and Garvin's voice whispered from its lips. "He is reporting that two Obrioner soldiers crashed through the gate."

"Who broke ranks?" Rory asked.

"No one."

Rory rose to peek through the canvas again just as Wolfram marched out, followed by the soldier.

He glanced back down at the nuall and Garvin spoke through it again. "Those two idiots, Tomas and Cameron, just rolled down the north peak. Crashed right through the front gate."

Rory glanced up at the steep cliff rising above the fort. He couldn't imagine how those two had ended up in Granadure, why they'd climb that peak, or what would possess them to crash the fort, but he didn't have time to wonder. He might not get another opportunity.

Slicing through the tent, Rory slipped inside and rushed to the table. The command tent wouldn't remain empty for long, but he only needed a moment.

He scanned the documents and maps, but he'd need an hour to sort through everything. He wasn't that fast at reading Obrioner to begin with, and Grandurian looked like gibberish to him.

Time seemed to fly on pedra's wings as he scanned the documents, and his muscles quivered with tension, but he fought the urge to tap granite. It took only a few seconds to realize what he had to do.

Rory swept every scrap of paper off the table and stuffed it all in the little leather satchel strapped to his battle jacket. He didn't have time to sort it all out, but Hector could assign some translators when Rory escaped back to Merkland.

He cast his eyes around the command tent to make sure he hadn't missed anything, and his eyes fell upon the wooden trunk at the end of the single, perfectly made camp cot nestled in an alcove across the tent. That had to belong to Wolfram.

Rory crossed the tent and couldn't help scratching a message with the tip of his dagger in the trunk.

With regards, Rory.

Grinning, Rory rushed back through the slit he'd made, escaped the tent, and ghosted back along the wall to the water barrels, then squirmed back under the wall. Garvin's nuall led him into the night where he rendezvoused with his men. They had approached to within thirty yards of the compound and looked relieved to see him.

"What is going on in there?" Rory demanded. "And where did those idiots come from?"

Garvin shrugged and chuckled. "I'm not even sure they realized they were invading an enemy fort. While you were stealing those papers, I watched the show. Those two were so busy pounding on each other, they barely seemed to notice the Grandurians. Something about an honor fight over a sister."

"I didn't know either of them had a sister."

"Who cares?" Garvin asked. "By the Tallan's crooked teeth, that surprise entry startled everyone. Those two somehow got the Grandurians to start cheering them on. Did you get what you needed?"

"Aye," Rory admitted.

A round of laughter echoed from the camp, and Rory frowned. "They can explain once we get them out of there."

"How do you propose we do that?" Garvin asked. "Weren't we supposed to avoid starting a war?"

Rory growled, "Working on it. Those two provided the distraction I needed, but now we need a distraction to get them out."

Macnab spoke up. "Sir, would a torc help?"

"A torc?" Rory asked. Most nights he'd feel surprised by such a bizarre question, but it somehow seemed perfectly appropriate with the way that night seemed to be going.

"Aye," Garvin said, flames dancing in his eyes. "Looks like those two idiots chained a torc before getting into their fight. It's right over there." He pointed to the right.

Rory grinned and clapped Garvin on the shoulder. "Lightning strikes the darkened mountain before the storm begins to rage."

Garvin frowned. "Your Sentry speak is terrible, sir."

"Probably for the best. Come on, men. I have an idea."

CHAPTER SIXTEEN

SECOND CHANCES

eneral Wolfram frowned at the two of them and spoke in clear, cultured Obrioner, with only a hint of an accent. "What is the meaning of this?"

Cameron exchanged a defiant look with Tomas. The two of them were panting, covered in dirt and sweat and nearly out of powder, but by the look in his eye, Tomas was just as willing as he was to fight the famous general.

"Doesn't mean nothing," Cameron said. "This is a private matter."

"Not when you take it to Grandurian soil."

"We're not finished, but if you want a turn, I'm happy to punch you down in front of your men," Tomas offered.

Wolfram's blue eyes twinkled, and his mustaches twitched, as if he nearly smiled. The mirth did not reach his eyes, and he said something in Grandurian. Many of his men laughed, although some began to frown at the pair, and Cameron wondered if the general had repeated Tomas's challenge.

"As much as I am interested in seeing the outcome of your quarrel, the presence of two Obrioners in my camp suggests there may be more in the area. I don't have time to play your game."

"Do you have time to eat my fist?" Cameron growled.

Wolfram gestured to the soldiers. "Bind them and prepare a scouting party."

Many of the soldiers looked disappointed, but they did not hesitate. As the men moved in, Tomas whipped the rope off his shoulder, tossed an end to Cameron, and shouted, "Grab on!"

Cameron did so, hoping Tomas had finally gotten a good idea. He had used up all of his already.

Tomas tapped granite and yanked on the rope, hauling Cameron into the air. Cameron shouted his favorite battle cry as Tomas swung him around like a living battering ram. Cameron locked his feet together, focusing his curse on his legs and knocking soldiers flying. The regulars tumbled away, and even the Rumblers paused in surprise.

With another rotation that spun Cameron even faster, Tomas released the rope, sending him soaring over the encircling soldiers. They should have used that move to cross the chasm. Tomas got great distance with it. Grinning, Cameron hit the ground and rolled, max-tapping granite and hauling mightily on the rope.

The angle was wrong to pull Tomas into the air, but he jumped as the rope tightened, and Cameron hauled so hard on the line that it sang with the tension. He was glad it didn't snap, but instead seemed to stretch, then rebounded the other way, yanking Tomas along and plowing him right through the ranks of startled Grandurians.

One Rumbler dove and tackled him, crashing the two of them to the ground nearby. Cameron lifted the Rumbler off and punched him so hard in the back of the neck that he cracked the skin. The man groaned and loosened his grip.

Cameron spun and launched the hapless Rumbler back into the ranks of his companions, scattering them again.

"We need to join the tumble-tosser team," Tomas grinned as he jumped to his feet and grabbed the rope again. He nodded toward the shattered gate. "One more time!"

"My turn. Hold on," Cameron said. He was nearly out of granite, which meant Tomas must be burning the last grains of his power. He made sure Tomas was holding the end of the rope, but he didn't have time to use it to throw him. Instead Cameron tapped deep from his waning supply of granite, linked arms with Tomas, and spun, throwing his partner over the soldiers blocking their escape route.

He missed the gate.

Tomas instead crashed into the stairs leading up to the walkway around the parapet on the left side of the gate. The angle actually worked better as Tomas tapped his curse and yanked on the rope, hauling Cameron through the air to crash onto the stairs beside him.

As Cameron bounded back to his feet, protected from the impact by his curse, Tomas slumped in obvious post-granite exhaustion. He'd burned his powder out.

"No sleeping yet," Cameron barked, lifting Tomas bodily to his feet. With Grandurian soldiers swarming after them, he wasn't sure they could jump off the stairs and escape out the smashed gate before getting overrun. So instead he tossed Tomas up the stairs to the walkway at the top of the parapet and scrambled after.

"That worked pretty good," Tomas said with a tired grin. "We're getting this teamwork thing figured out."

"Took you long enough," Cameron said with an answering grin.

It was definitely time to go. Facing the company of charging Grandurians with a fully powered curse would have been a dream come true. Facing them with a weakened partner and his own curse nearly spent was a nightmare.

Before they could leap over the palisade and escape into the night, flames erupted out of thin air, blocking their path in a rippling wall of fire.

"Flameweaver," Tomas growled as intense heat drove them back a step.

Cameron spun to locate the threat. A Flameweaver was even worse than facing Rumblers with barely any granite. Those deadly tertiaries could roast a man to charred meat in seconds, even through the protection of granite. The only chance against them was to close fast and overwhelm them before they could unleash their deadly fire.

A tall man with flames dancing in his hair stood atop the wall on the opposite side of the smashed gate. Flames danced around his head in a crimson halo.

"We'll never get through to that one," Cameron growled, and saw his own fear reflected in Tomas's eyes.

Down in the courtyard, Wolfram clapped twice, drawing their gaze.

"I admire your resourcefulness, gentlemen, but surrender and get down here, or I will have no choice but to order your incineration."

"What does that mean?" Cameron whispered.

Tomas shrugged. "He's an Allcarver. Must be a new kind of torture."

"You have two seconds," Wolfram shouted, and in that moment he looked every inch the implacable general Cameron had heard about. He stood tall, one hand on his sword, expression hard as granite.

"We might be in trouble," Cameron suggested.

Tomas grunted agreement. "Even your girlfriend's frying pan would help. I could throw it at the general. Even that much would help."

Help came in the form of a flying torc.

The huge beast that had led them on such an epic hunt all evening soared out of the darkness beyond the outpost without warning. Bellowing with rage, as if someone had kicked it between the legs before tossing it, the huge animal slammed into the Flameweaver, and the two of them tumbled off the wall. They struck the ground so hard that a cloud of dust erupted from the point of impact.

The enraged torc rolled to its feet and charged the mass of nearby soldiers, scattering them and impaling one poor fellow on its long, bent horn. The man's scream startled Cameron out of his shocked immobility.

"That's our torc!" he exclaimed.

"We trained it better than I thought," Tomas said, watching with approval as the torc trampled four regulars too slow to dodge its charge.

"But that's our second chance," Cameron protested.

Tomas pointed over the palisade wall. "That's the only second chance we're getting tonight. Let's get out of here!"

Another good idea in as many minutes. Tomas was risking post-thinking exhaustion on top of his post-granite fatigue. The man was throwing caution to the wind. Cameron heartily approved.

The wall of fire blocking their escape had snuffed out. In fact, the Flameweaver hadn't moved since he'd gotten squashed into the ground by a thousand pounds of angry torc.

Cameron crouched to jump over, but noticed Tomas hesitate. He was probably afraid of breaking legs not protected by granite when he landed. So Cameron threw him high into the air over the edge. He jumped after, but without the high additional arc and landed first. As Tomas fell, limbs flailing, shouting curses at him, he caught his partner by the battle leathers and swung him, transferring his fall into a horizontal flight that sent him tumbling across the grass and into the concealing night.

Bowling Tomas was a lot of fun, and it helped ease Cameron's anger at the loss of the torc he'd spent so much time and effort hunting. Now it seemed they would have to start all over again, save a new powder store, and plan another hunt.

Tomas came unsteadily to his feet as Cameron caught up to him. Cameron pointed him in the right direction and pushed him forward. As they ran into the protective darkness, Cameron wondered about the torc. They'd left it chained up. How had it managed to untie itself? Even though it was an Obrioner torc, he'd never heard torcs were known to attack Grandurians, and he'd never imagined the huge beast could jump so high. There was more to torcs than the hunt master had told him.

A soft, greenish limelight ignited nearby, illuminating Sergeant Rory and his squad of black-clad Fast Rollers.

Cameron and Tomas halted in front of Rory and snapped simultaneous salutes.

"What are you doing out here, Sergeant?" Tomas asked.

"I might ask you the same thing," Rory replied, his craggy face betraying nothing of what he might be thinking.

"Don't worry about them Grandurians," Cameron said, jabbing a finger back at the compound they had just fled. The sounds of shouting had died down, and no doubt their brave torc had been subdued, but he doubted pursuit would be quick to follow.

Rory chuckled. "How do you think you escaped?"

"You threw our torc?" Tomas asked, making the connection a split second before Cameron did.

"Of course. I couldn't pass up such a perfect distraction, could I?"

"Just why we left it there," Cameron said quickly. They'd lost their second chance, but if Rory was impressed by the beast they'd caught, maybe the night wasn't a total loss.

"I'm sure," Rory said, although by his tone it was clear he wasn't. "Move out."

As the company trotted through the darkness back toward the bridge over the border chasm and Obrioner soil, Cameron realized something.

"You threw that torc, sir. So you had to see it flying."

"Indeed. It seems at times that torcs really do fly."

Tomas grinned. "Guess that means we proved ourselves, right Sergeant?"

Rory sighed. "I can't believe I'm saying this, but yes, your actions tonight helped me complete my mission. You've won your second chance."

Cameron exchanged a grin with Tomas, but then frowned. "Both of us? Are you sure you want to give a blockheaded flatlander like Tomas another chance?"

"Who punched Albin hard enough to prove his tap-rate management idea works?"

"But do you remember to put your pants on before your boots?"

Tomas mumbled something that sounded like, "Most days."

Cameron added, "And your breath is so bad, the cook uses it to curdle milk."

"She just wants an excuse to spend time with me."

Rory rolled his eyes. "Enough. You both get your second chance, and Tomas is no longer a flatlander. He's one of us."

Tomas looked ridiculously pleased, and Cameron clapped him on the shoulder in congratulations. He wouldn't admit it, but he would miss beating on Tomas every day.

"You two are partners, so get used to each other's company," Rory finished.

"You can't be serious," Cameron complained out of habit.

Tomas said, "No one else can stand you. Guess I'm the strongest after all."

"Ha! You're assigned to me only 'cause Sergeant knows I'm the only one who can whip you into shape."

"Enough," Rory growled again. "Or I'll assign you both to study Sentry speak with Gregor."

The two of them fell silent, although Cameron could see the insults building behind Tomas's eyes. He was already working on a score of new ones to counter his partner. He was shocked to realize he was looking forward to the next exchange. Tomas could hold his own better than anyone he knew.

As the company trotted across the bridge, Cameron couldn't suppress a happy grin.

He had his second chance. He would win a place among the Fast Rollers. And he'd get to insult Tomas every day for at least a week.

He couldn't imagine Rory would leave the two of them together for longer than that.

Petralist Stones

Igneous

Basalt
Speed, agility
Tapped: Powder
through theskin
Obrion: Strider
Granadure:Wingrunner

Granite
Strength, summoning
Tapped: Powder
through the skin
Obrion: Boulder or
Fast Roller
Granadure:
Rumbler

Obsidian
Magnifies innate abilities
Tapped: Powder through the skin
Obrion: Blade
Granadure: Allcarver

SEDIMENTARY

Limestone
Light
Tapped: Held or worn
Obrion: Solas
Granadure: Solas

Sandstone
Healing
Tapped: Held or worn
Obrion: Healer
Granadure: Healer

METAMORPHIC

Marble
Fire
Tapped: Under the Tongue
Obrion: Firetongue
Granadure: Flameweaver

Slate
Earth
Tapped: Soles of feet
Obrion: Sentry
Granadure: Sapper

Quartzite
Air, Senses
Tapped: Placed in Mouth
Obrion: Pathfinder
Granadure: Longseer

Soapstone
Water
Tapped: Swallowedwith water
Obrion: Spitter
Granadure: Water Moccasin

New Stones!

Diorite
Igneous Stone
Explosive Power
Tapped: Powder through the skin
Obrion: Unknown
Granadure: Unknown

Porphyry
Igneous Stone
Rage Monster
Tapped: Powder through the skin
Obrion: Unclaimed
Granadure: Rampager

Anthracite (Blind Coal)
Sedimentary Stone
Aggressive Slipperiness
Tapped: Held or worn
Obrion: Unknown
Granadure: Unknown

Serpentinite
Metamorphic Stone
Sound
Tapped: Unknown
Obrion: Unknown
Granadure: Unknown

Author's Note

If you enjoyed this book, please tell people about it. Blog about it, tell all your friends, buy copies for everyone who lives in your city - whatever you feel is enough to share how much fun you had reading this book.

This one was particularly fun to write.

Reviews help more than you know, particularly on Amazon. They directly help the book become more visible, which is the best way you can support me, one of your favorite authors.

Thank you!

Since you've read all the way through the dreaded, boring author's note, you're a super fan, and I thank you again. Please share your suggestions for the next non-main-series Petralist book and get involved in my Reader's Group newsletter.

Thank you!

Really, I mean it. I hope you return to my imaginary worlds often.

And of course, you're already asking, "When is the next book coming out?"

As soon as I possibly can!

Acknowledgements

When Torcs Fly is the first book in the Petralist world not part of the main series, and it definitely won't be the last. This book was born during a meeting with my Story Squad team in my living room over ice cream sundaes. Like Hamish, we think better when we're eating.

In particular, thanks to my enthusiastic family and the die-hard core of the group: Matt Hattrick, Ben Rivas, and Zach Huff.

In the past, we had focused on the big works in progress, but with that meeting we began exploring side stories and ways to expand the Petralist world outside of the main series. I proposed a simple question: "Where should we start. Whose story do you want?"

Everyone wanted Kilian of course, but enough of his back-story is already coming out in *Affinity for War* that we couldn't focus on that yet. The universal second choice was Tomas and Cameron. These hilarious supporting characters are some of the most popular characters outside of the central core, and we laughed for an hour and a half as we brainstormed how these two goofy bash fighters might have started out.

The result is *When Torcs Fly*, and everyone should raise a sweetbread in honor of the Story Squad. Without their help, who knows what we would have ended up with.

In addition to Story Squad, I owe thanks to Joshua Essoe, the brilliant editor whose brutally honest feedback helped shape this story, just as it has every other Petralist book. And Kathryn Renta produced a brilliant cover that exactly fits the story, and which ties in beautifully with the covers of the main series.

What story is next in the non-main-series Petralist world? We've already outlined a super-fun story about Anika's brief but memorable stint as a florist!

But I'll ask each of you the same question: "Whose story do you want next?"

Contact me with your ideas on my Facebook page or my website, and Story Squad will include your recommendations as we plan the next one.

Other Works by Frank Morin

The Petralist Series

Set in Stone - Book One
A Stone's Throw - Book Two
No Stone Unturned - Book Three
Affinity for War - Book Four (release date: May 2018)

Other Petralist Stories

When Torcs Fly – Tomas and Cameron prequel (you're reading it!)

The Facetakers Series

Face Lift - Prequel short story
Saving Face - Prequel
Memory Hunter - Book One
Rune Warrior - Book Two
Aeon Champion - Book Three: coming soon

Short Stories

Odin's Eye - Part of the Red Unicorn Anthology - *A Game of Horns*
Only Logical - Part of *Unseen: United! Box Set* Anthology to raise funds to fight plagiarism
The Essence - Part of the *Dragon Writers* Anthology (Release date in Q4 2016)

About the Author

Frank Morin is a storyteller, and he loves great stories wherever he can find them. When not writing or trying to keep up with his active family, he's often found hiking, camping, Scuba diving, or enjoying other outdoor activities.

Frank writes all types of fantasy, from his exciting Facetakers contemporary fantasy / time-travel thrillers, to these popular Petralist novels, and more. Check his website for updates and to sign up for his newsletter to receive the latest on all his releases, scheduled events, and insider information: www.frankmorin.org.

Or you can follow him on Twitter:
@MorinWrites
Or like his Author Facebook page:
www.facebook.com/authorfrankmorin

Frank lives in Oregon with his family, who are his most enthusiastic fans and his most brutal critics. In their home, storytelling is a cherished family tradition that keeps magic alive.